Short
Candles

Short
Candles

Rita Donovan

darkstar
f i c t i o n

Cover art/design: Vasiliki Lenis
Author photo: Ryszard Mrugalski

Le Conseil des Arts | The Canada Council
DU CANADA | FOR THE ARTS
DEPUIS 1957 | SINCE 1957

RendezVous Press acknowledges the support of the Canada Council for our publishing program.

Darkstar Fiction
An imprint of Napoleon and Company
Toronto, Ontario, Canada
www.napoleonandcompany.com

11 10 09 08 07   5 4 3 2 1

Library and Archives Canada Cataloguing in Publication

Donovan, Rita, date-
    Short candles / Rita Donovan.

ISBN 978-1-894917-53-7

    I. Title.
PS8557.O58S56 2007   C813'.54   C2007-903848-4

For Carol, For Tony

Well, it's all right,
Love is what you want.
Flying saucer, take me away,
Give me your daughter.
                    -Marc Bolan, T.Rex

Fire Engine Sue

If she is wearing the shoes with the straps, do not look for the perfect punch hole her father has added with his awl. It is there, but hidden beneath the twisted posy of yellow trefoil and purple cow vetch with which she decorates her shoes.

Little Sue Cardinal, who will carry "little" until she is older, like Little Stevie Wonder, the blind singer she does not know, takes the route by the river nearly every day. It is the 1960s, and her parents are not worried about abduction, or drowning, or evil people who would take a child from a pathway and destroy it. Her parents are worried about other things: her father Robert, his health, which has magically declined, as if someone has a curse on him; and her mother Adele, her job working in an office on the other side of town.

Besides, everyone knows that Fire Engine Sue can take care of herself. Look at how confidently she skips along the trail, as if she has memorized every rock, every grassy clump of earth. She has been referred to as Fire Engine Sue since she was four years old and awoke to warn her family of a fire that was just beginning to lick up the yellow curtains in the kitchen. There was significant damage to their well-appointed house, but the family was safe, and everyone agreed that it could have been much, much worse. The baby, Carla, was in her crib, and everyone knew how smoke affected babies. It was Suzanne, Little Sue, Fire Engine Sue, who had saved them.

This is the beginning of it then. For it is one thing to wake up to the smell of smoke, to be a light sleeper, perhaps, or slightly weak of bladder. It is another to be able to tell the future. At four, the future is just about everything, her father argues at night with his wife. Why do people come to her with their problems? For Suzanne is what every community wants, an amulet against chaos.

Nothing is supposed to break through the line of box elders and maples at the edge of town. Why do you think those rows of peonies and the tall cosmos are along the driveways? And now they have Fire Engine Sue to keep them one step ahead of calamity, the law, the cancer creeping up the spine.

The town prides itself on those lines of trees along the perimeter. It had been a group endeavour some twenty years earlier, when people came back from the war. Suzanne's father had come back then too, almost as young as when he'd left, but not as fresh. No. He was nineteen when he returned, having joined up with parental permission. Too young to drink or vote when he had enlisted, he had nonetheless managed to maneuver his tank across parts of Holland, to the relief of the thin and ragged Dutch. Or so he said.

He doesn't talk much about the war any more. It is tucked into the headband of his fedora like a feather. And who is wearing hats these days?

Suzanne stops skipping, for there is a bullfrog

speaking to her from the edge of the river. The bank is low here, so she goes over and waits politely for him to complete his original composition before continuing on. She should do something today. She wants to build a shelter in the woods for lost penguins, but she is unsure of the dimensions of such a structure. She will go to the library. They have everything there, books about people's throats, a story about a wagon train that stretches far back into the picture on the cover. They will know about penguins as well.

"Hello, Little Sue!"

Mrs. Reidel. She is hanging out the same tablecloth again. The berry stain has not come out, despite the expensive powder she bought at Laturelle's store. It has faded, though, into a light and pleasing pink that reminds Suzanne of the cheeks of her doll, Annabelle.

"Hello!" she waves back. "The bullfrog talked again."

"Good," Mrs. Reidel says, shaking a pale green dishtowel out of the basket. "Could you hand me some pins?"

Suzanne is over the fence in a flash and pointing wooden clothespins at Mrs. Reidel.

"They look like crocodiles."

"Hmmm?"

The pins are in Mrs. Reidel's mouth, four crocodiles ready to snap.

"Do you know about penguin houses?"

What people cannot understand, then, what has them really puzzled, is the cruelty of the gift. Little Sue, Fire Engine Sue, successfully predicted Mr. Gaumper's broken leg, on ice in front of Laturelle's store. She was able to warn Bobby Allerton away from three possible allergic reactions, one deadly. She told people to cover their plants, and Mrs. Reidel was one of the few who listened, and therefore did not lose her crop of tomatoes and beets to the freak hailstorm only four weeks earlier.

So what people have trouble understanding is how such a gift could not have prevented tiny Carla from falling to her death. Really, this sentiment almost overtook the general dismay at the funeral two years ago. Here was a baby who had survived a house fire, a toddler who followed her sister Suzanne around like a trusty St. Bernard. Suzanne knew this child better, surely, than she knew Mr. Gaumper's leg or Bobby Allerton's allergies, and yet the toddler was found beneath the second floor balcony, her small precise bones shaken and jittered back into place.

Robert Cardinal blamed himself. Hadn't he been told to watch the tot that afternoon? Adele Cardinal blamed him as well. Suzanne? She said Carla was flying to Jesus and had left her body, with the scabbed knee, behind.

"Jesus might not like scabs."

People kept away from Little Sue for a while after that. Perhaps the town didn't have its own Fire Engine after all. Maybe it was a fluke. After all, it was inevitable that somebody would break a leg outside Laturelle's store; the guy never salted or sanded.

Over time, a few people came back. Suzanne never refused to speak with anyone. And if they brought along a sucker or a bag of caramels, well, so much the · better. Most people, though, just thought of her as the strange little kid who had lost her sister, an unfortunate blip in the timeline of the town.

"Hello Mrs. Craig," Suzanne says as she bounces past the desk.

"Ssshhh." The hand points to the SILENCE sign, as it always does when Suzanne arrives at the library. Mrs. Craig sighs. It isn't the child's fault. She's a wildflower, that one. Where are her parents? Why doesn't anyone take the child in hand?

Suzanne studies the grass stain on her knee before diving into the stacks of books. It is a nice pattern, like sun on a field of green. Sprinkled. Blurry.

"No scabs, Carla," she whispers to her knee.

The first time they took Suzanne to the optometrist, he said, "There's nothing wrong with her eyes." She had correctly identified not only the letters on the chart that Dr. Marsh had pulled down over his bookshelf, but the letters on the books behind it as well.

"Could you…" he pulled out a bottle of pills and had her read the fine print. "Just spell it if you can't say the words."

And Suzanne read the dosage and side effects for Dr. Marsh.

"Thank you. Damn little labels."

Adele Cardinal had taken the morning off work for this and stood facing Dr. Marsh, holding her daughter's head between her hands as if to steady it.

"But she says she sees blurs."

He put his hand under Suzanne's chin and lifted. They were arguing over her head.

"You don't see anything blurry, do you, Little Sue?"

"Only when things are blurry."

"There you are," Dr. Marsh smiled.

Adele Cardinal couldn't believe it. Maybe she was going crazy.

Her life has not gone well these last years. Oh, no. How does one survive the death of a child, a perfect child who caused no trouble or worry, a child who brought only happiness, and no confusion, to the home? It was such a comfort to see her in her pink flared coat and bonnet, a new garment, not a hand-me-down from Suzanne. The child had dark curls and an open expression devoid of the quizzical squint of her older sister. She was a joy, and that joy had found a way to turn the latch on the balcony door, toddle out past the wicker chair and petunias, and fling itself away. Joy. Gone. The door bumping open and shut.

It is not the same between her and Robert any more. How could it be? He is constantly distracted. Robert writes in his "must-do" ledger, yet the more he plans, the less he does.

He will wash the car.

But the car stands there in the driveway, a permanent taupe colour, the grime thick with loss and Suzanne's printed "Hello."

And so. What is there for Adele but the offices of Honoré & Stevens? What else except typing up wills and property settlements, the who-gets-what of deaths and divorces? You are miserable? You are in despair? Here, you may have a duplex.

Absurd, she tells herself in triplicate, as she carries the papers in to be signed.

Supper. Suzanne is putting raisin climbers on the side of the mountain of mashed potatoes. A trail of brown sugar and ketchup is edging down the other side.

"Look out, look out! What is it called again?"

Suzanne's father looks over with his absent eyes. "Lava," he whispers.

"Lava," Suzanne nods, as the raisins unknowingly head toward doom.

This cannot go on. Adele has been resisting the offer to send Suzanne to Sophie's. The child likes her Aunt Sophie well enough, but Adele is not convinced her sister truly understands what it is like caring for Fire Engine Sue.

"Just the summer. What can it do? I'm alone here since Vince is gone. I have the time. Send her to me. You and Robert can have some time of your own together."

Adele bites her lip.

Then she thinks of Suzanne, wandering the town by herself all day, probably bored to tears.

"Yes, yes, okay. Next Saturday." She hangs up but keeps the phone in her lap, and gently pets it, like a cat.

"This is too small," Adele admonishes, throwing a pair of pedal-pushers and a pop-top onto the floor. "And this?" She holds it before Suzanne's slender body. "Yes. Finished."

The child watches as the pile grows at her feet.

"When did this happen?" her mother demands, as if it is spilled sugar that is drawing ants.

"I don't know," the child replies. She looks down at her legs then holds out her arms. "Do you think it's perm-mament?"

Adele is forced to drag Suzanne down to the only dry goods store in town, where summer outfits hang on pegboards in the window. One Sunday dress, green. Three sets of shorts and tops. Suzanne points to the pink set with puppies on it.

"Linda has that. And Cassie. I'll look like twins," the child says.

Back at home, the small suitcase with the cloth-embroidered flowers is filling up. A bathing suit is thrown in. Who knows if it fits? It is when she sees her lamb go in, her battered lamb that survived the fire and her sister's pulling, that she starts to cry.

"Oh, what now? It will be fun for you. Aunt Sophie has time to take you to the zoo, and the park. She'll even read to you."

Suzanne curls up in her mother's arms, and Adele holds her while trying to take the tangled elastic out of her hair.

"If I go, Mrs. Reidel will die," Suzanne whispers to her mother's thighs.

She must warn Mrs. Reidel to be very, very careful while she is away. She doesn't want to scare her, but she must tell her all the same. Suzanne throws on her new dress, slips out on Saturday morning, and runs, runs, runs along the path by the house. Nobody is outside. The trucks are quiet. The dogs and birds are awake, but she notices the peacefulness of the morning and slows her pace a moment. The trees overhead make a green ceiling, but if you look up, you can see the sun behind them. And then—quick—she runs until she sees the pale yellow house. The tomatoes are well. The beet greens wave at her like always.

She knocks at the screen door.

Mrs. Reidel likes to get up early, but not this early. Suzanne listens. No toaster popping, no coffee percolating, no cat whining for his breakfast. Too early. She will be in trouble again. She runs around the side of the house. Mrs. Reidel's big hollyhocks are in the way. Suzanne looks around. There, on the ground, the small flat ladder the old woman walks across on muddy days to get to her toolshed.

Suzanne bends and lifts one end. Too heavy. She pulls with all her might and drags it across the yard, over to the hollyhocks.

"Sorry, flowers," she says. She is a little afraid of the hollyhocks. They loom. No time to worry now, though, and she tips the ladder up against the side of the house. She climbs, feeling the flowers scratching her legs. She is *in* the hollyhocks. Suzanne puts her hands on the window frame and peers in. The filmy white curtains make everything hazy, but she can make out the dresser and the bed over to the right. Mrs. Reidel is definitely in the bed, her large body covered in pale blue. Suzanne wonders if the tea stain is still on the coverlet. The window is open a crack to let in air. To let in only small insects. Suzanne can fit her fingers under it, so she does then yanks up. The force nearly topples her from the ladder.

More space. For bigger insects. Or, if she just…ouch!…now. Yes. Big enough for her. Suzanne climbs up on the sill and slips her legs in. The drop to the floor is not great, and she plops down almost silently. Ferg the cat looks up from the bed and starts to scowl, but seeing who it is, turns away contentedly.

"Hi Ferg," Suzanne says quietly. She tiptoes over to the bed. Of course, Mrs. Reidel is asleep. It is early Saturday morning. If Suzanne wakes her, she will be in trouble.

"Mrs. Reidel," she shakes gently. "Mrs...Mrs. Reidel." Her voice gets stronger as the woman does not move or mutter. The cat has sprung to the floor in the commotion and now adds his voice to the chorus.

Suzanne saw something once on television, so she goes to the bathroom and gets the small lipstick-stained cup from its stand above the sink, and fills it with water. Back at the bedside, she crosses the fingers of her free hand and throws the water into Mrs. Reidel's face.

Nothing.

The cat is meowing. Suzanne runs down the hall to the telephone table. She remembers the numbers and watches the dial spinning slowly, too slowly, around each time.

Three rings. Four. And on the fifth ring, her father's voice.

"Come! Help!" she says, her eyes on the hallway.

The ambulance arrives with Suzanne's parents. Her father looks funny in his casual trousers and pyjama top. Her mother has her hair in curlers beneath a printed scarf. She pulls Suzanne to her in a gesture that is somewhere between fear and anger. The stretcher is sliding down the hall now. Suzanne closes her eyes.

"Is it?" her mother asks. "Is she?"

The ambulance attendant looks up. "Where's the girl?"

She is hiding behind her mother.

"Fire Engine Sue, you came just in time. Diabetic coma," he adds, nodding to Mrs. Cardinal.

Suzanne rides home in the car. They have not told her. Does this mean Mrs. Reidel will live? They have not said anything about how she crept out of her home and crawled into the window of Mrs. Reidel's house. They have not scolded her for the rip in her brand new, green Sunday dress that she is wearing on Saturday to go to the city. Suzanne flicks open the miniature metal ashtray in the back seat armrest and studies the ledge, where a cigarette gets to sit and watch the world of ash below.

•

Aunt Sophie's house is in a residential section of the city, but buses at the end of the street can take them anywhere they want to go. The library, which is a giant grown-up version of Mrs. Craig's library back home, has more children's books than Suzanne has ever seen before. How can a child read so many books? And there is the ice cream parlour with dozens of flavours, and the spruce doggie on the corner, a sad-looking terrier who seems to live beneath the spruce tree. Aunt Sophie tells Suzanne that she has never seen the dog anywhere but under that tree.

"It's his tree house," Suzanne replies.

Sophie Marsala has been widowed almost a year. Vince was her second husband, and both husbands succumbed to heart attacks.

"Maybe it's Sophie's cooking," Suzanne's father joked at the table soon after Vince died.

Suzanne's eyes widen as she remembers this. Aunt Sophie is passing her a plate of spaghetti. She is hungry. Didn't her stomach rumble all the way home on the bus? The meatballs are small and perfectly round. The sauce looks okay. What about that sprinkle of cheese? Suzanne knows how Alice felt wondering which drink she wasn't supposed to eat or drink. But this isn't Wonderland, and Suzanne says a little prayer to Jesus to save her from poison meatballs then digs in.

Nothing.

Tasty.

Suzanne smiles at her aunt, now cutting poison bread and pouring poison milk. There. They click glasses, Suzanne's milk spills onto her spaghetti, and they both laugh.

Unlike Suzanne's mother's hair, Aunt Sophie's is long and wound up in a bun. There is grey hair and black hair mixed together. Suzanne likes how the hair moves like a wave when she undoes it.

Aunt Sophie combs out Suzanne's tangles, too, and they sit side by side, looking into the mirror.

"Tell me, Little Sue, what does the future hold for your old aunt?"

She is only a little bit joking, for she has stopped combing and is staring right at her reflection.

But of course, this is not how it goes. Suzanne can no more say what will become of Aunt Sophie than she can say what will become of Suzanne.

"Did you know…did you know about Uncle Vince?"

There is a look on Aunt Sophie's face. She holds the comb strangely. Suzanne closes her eyes for a moment and shivers. When she opens them, Aunt Sophie is dabbing her eyes with a tissue.

Adele calls to see how they are getting on. Suzanne tells her mother that Aunt Sophie is the cheerfullest person she knows. Then Adele talks to Sophie. Suzanne cannot understand the half-conversation, so she goes out back to see the worms. Even though this is the city, there are piles of earth here and there in the yard. There is one pile that Aunt Sophie says used to belong to a tree. The tree was removed, but the earth stayed, and now Suzanne can visit the worms there.

"Worthworms," she says at supper that evening.

Aunt Sophie looks up from her plate. "You mean earthworms?"

"Worthworms. They're really hard workers. They're worth a lot."

Aunt Sophie wants to give Suzanne a kitten. "Something to love," she explains to Adele. Something to keep her busy? Better a dog, then, to romp with through the woods. A cat will sit and stare and not allow itself to be played with by a schoolgirl who speaks to bullfrogs. It will not be a pet.

"You know, a pet!" Sophie pleads.

But where is Little Sue? Why is she not begging and carrying on as children are supposed to when the issue of small animals is raised? Why is it Sophie who whimpers and grovels?

Little Sue is in Aunt Sophie's backyard talking to the worms.

"Really, Adele, a cat or a dog. Right away."

Soon, however, the summer is over. The cool evening breezes of August brush the tiny hairs on Suzanne's arms and tell her soon. *Soon. Snow.*

It is so cold one evening that Aunt Sophie lights a fire in the fireplace. Suzanne breathes deep. Burning wood. Clean wood, not like the smell of her house when it was in flames. Soon she will leave and return to

town for school. She will be in Grade Two. She will find
her tunic and slip it over her head. Will it fit? She holds
out her arms. She can never see herself growing, but
they tell her she is.

She must see Charlie Donaldson. She must tell him
about the train bridge.

"Mommy?" The phone is heavy.

Suzanne hears the sigh in her mother's voice. "What
is it? You have two days left with your aunt."

"Mommy? Could you tell Charlie Donaldson not to
go on the train bridge? He likes to go on the train
bridge with his brother, and he can't, okay?"

This is not what parents should have to put up with.
Adele has her monthly pains and has already flown off
the handle at work today. She does not need this kind
of nonsense. So she reassures the child, hangs up the
phone and goes to lie down on the couch.

Suzanne does a jigsaw puzzle with Aunt Sophie. A
clown in a little racing car, with a monkey balancing on
his head.

"I have the monkey's wave!" Suzanne cries.

While on a trestle, in the setting sun, Charlie
Donaldson dies.

•

Time passes, blue trickles in the stream. Except that
when Suzanne holds the water in her hand, it is clear.
She wonders about water, how far it travels, not only
downstream but up into the air and down again. They
are learning that in school. It never disappears, not
really; it just becomes something else.

Mrs. Reidel is in a wheelchair, and her flowers are dusty. Suzanne has given up pulling weeds and spends the afternoons practicing her reading with Mrs. Reidel. The woman seems so much older, although it has only been months since the summer. She likes to hear Little Sue read, or so she says. They both like *The Snow Queen*. Mrs. Reidel says she knew someone once whose heart was frozen like Kay's was in the story.

"Did the boy have a Gerda?" A little girl to search for him, to find him and melt his frozen heart?

Mrs. Reidel smiles from her wheelchair, Ferg curled up in her lap. "Yes. Yes, there was a girl."

A whole term goes by, then a blurry Christmas, and soon there is an Easter Egg Hunt in Mrs. Reidel's garden, but all Suzanne finds are clothespins and poo from the dog next door. Mrs. Reidel presents her with a chocolate bunny, the largest Suzanne has seen. They keep it at Mrs. Reidel's house and eat from it after school, even though Mrs. Reidel's doctor says she can't. When they are down to the toes—hooves? pads?—of the bunny, school is ready to end again. It is the beginning of something that will be called "The Summer of Love". Suzanne does not listen to the radio and doesn't hear about the young people, their clothes, the crazy music. She is down by the river.

"I love the summer," she tells the bullfrog. "Of course, you do, too."

Her parents are busy. Her father is taking care of his health by running around. He puts on his baggy shorts and a T-shirt, and he runs around in the basement. He doesn't want to go outside yet, he says, because of his form. Suzanne looks at her father. He is formed like her father, long skinny legs coming out of the enormous leg holes of his shorts, long torso and his turtle head on top. He runs around until he gets tired, then he flops down on the old sofa with the sticking-out spring at the end. He lies there for a while before getting up and running around again.

"What are you doing?"

"Trying to stay alive," he gasps.

And runs in the basement like the well pump.

.

It is sometimes strange to believe that it could really be true, that Little Sue could really be Fire Engine Sue, a girl with a gift. This child cannot even make her bed properly. She is a bright but indifferent student. How can she possess the abilities they claim?

For they do come to her. Mrs. Reidel sends for her, but they are old friends. Yet some still trek up the Cardinals' driveway, on the flimsy excuse of borrowing flour, toting a small gift for Suzanne.

"I want to buy the coffee shop. Should I go ahead and do it?"

"Is Michael Cormack the right man for me?"

"Will I ever quit smoking?"

It doesn't matter how many times Adele or Suzanne tell them, they return, sheepishly, to the front door, always embarrassed, always with questions.

If the child had any powers, wouldn't she tell Adele? Couldn't Adele benefit from knowing, just a little in advance, the many trials she must endure? In the newspapers, they are speaking about new consciousness, about opening up your mind. Could this be what they mean? Has Suzanne become like the hippies out on the city streets, running off to India and ingesting things that cause them to have visions? Taking LSD and trying to fly off the edges of buildings, only to fall...

Truth be told, Adele is afraid of the young people on the street. They unnerve her with their colourful long skirts, their wild peasant blouses and bouncing breasts, their hair that looks like birds have nested in it. They kiss in public, with tongues. They sing when they feel like it. And they seem to hate Adele, who dresses in pastel pantsuits that are neat, unwrinkled and clean.

Suzanne is but a child. She has no part in this "new consciousness". And Adele aims to see that it stays that way.

"No more make-believe. No more pretend. No more talking to animals."

"You talk to Fidel," Suzanne says.

The dog out front of Cormier's bakery.

"No waiting for them to talk back," her mother says.

It is hard to imagine a world of such silence. Suzanne hears thunder in her ears as she walks the river path. No voices, no sounds addressing her. She is mute in a loud and undifferentiated world in which dolls are dolls and worms are wordless.

How can people live in such loneliness?

"I'm telling you, Suzanne, go out and find a friend. Make friends with Jeremy."

The boy down the road. Jeremy is eight, but already he has mastered how to burn insects with his brother's magnifying glass. Already he chops worms into bits with his penknife. He plays marbles to win. He cheats at checkers. She will not go there.

"You don't want to become a hermit, do you?"

A hermit crab walking sideways across the carpet of the sea bottom, snapping his claws? Or a hermit like the one Father Jacques told her about once, who lived with the bugs and insects and talked to air.

"I'm worried about her," Adele tells Robert as they sit at the kitchen table. Little Sue has padded downstairs and is listening by the door. She can peek through the doorjamb.

Robert shrugs and runs his fingers through his turtle hair. "I've tried to talk to you about having another one..."

But Adele will hear none of it. There is no way she will entrust another of her children to this family of careless people. It was carelessness that took Carla from her mother's arms.

"My carelessness!" Suzanne hears her father's anguished voice.

"Yes! You and that child, who was supposed to be a big sister, who goes about warning and saving other people but..."

She chokes off the rest. There it is, then. Fire Engine Sue. Fire Engine Sue and Adele's useless husband, the reasons Carla died.

Adele and Robert have been to this place before and somehow always manage to pull themselves back, with half-hearted promises and grief. They even apologize once in a while and resolve not to let their daughter's name enter into their problems. But tonight Suzanne hears none of the making up, for she has crept back to her room to lie beneath the rumpled bedspread. The moon is lighting part of her wall, on the side of the room where Carla would have slept.

"I'm sorry," she whispers to the night, wet tears sliding down into her ears.

.

She is old enough to know that the girl who owns the nail polish is in charge. Joanne Albert has her sister's leftover bottles of nail polish and scabbed tubes of lipstick. Once a week, the entrepreneur gathers the makeup into a basket and comes around looking for shoppers. She says she is the Avon lady, but she looks nothing like the heavily made-up woman with the wig who brings Suzanne's mother samples. Joanne is supplier to kids like Suzanne who have developed a sudden interest in these pots and tubes. Often they will meet at the big tree in the park, three or four girls with cuts on their shins, stains on their knees. When Joanne has her juvenile coven primed, she opens, slowly, the first bottle of nail polish.

"Blushing Rose," she intones, to the girls' collective intake of breath. "It is fresh and dis-cree."

Suzanne almost proffers a nail of her own then holds back, remembering the other bottles in the basket.

Joanne sweeps a bottle through the air. "Torrid Tango...for those hot, hot nights."

Suzanne cannot possibly imagine how one red fingernail is going to provide relief from the sweaty summer evenings. The polish has obscured her cuticle and is only slightly covering the hangnail she's been chewing.

"Beautiful," she says quietly, but Joanne hears it.

"Forty cents for the rest of the bottle."

Suzanne doesn't have forty cents. She has only twenty-six cents: two dimes and six pennies, and one of those pennies is a flat railroad penny. Besides, Suzanne cannot trade away her entire holdings for one item, no matter how wonderful. So she shakes her head and gets up from under the tree. She can hear Joanne going on about a small and stinky bottle of perfume, but she is leaving. She has fended off the need and is happy with her red fingernail, the pointer of her left hand, pointing her home.

"I am entirely in love," she murmurs, lying on her stomach on the big rock by the river, crossing her eyes and staring at the scarlet glow of her finger. Water moves over the stones, and the afternoon disappears downriver.

·

It doesn't happen for a long time after that. Suzanne is immersed in school, in her classes that go on all day long, with Mrs. Naylor walking up and down the aisles, a ruler in her hand. Slap, slap, the ruler says, as she moves past every desk. And on one of these passes Suzanne feels it, the slight push like someone's hand has found her lower back and is nudging her forward.

It is the feeling of knowing, and Suzanne tries to shake it off, to place her attention on the sums in front of her, but the numbers dance before her eyes, the sevens and the fives, the threes ballooning, blowing across the page.

"Mrs. Naylor," she speaks softly, to herself. "Mrs. Naylor." The roving woman stops, takes a step or two back and is now standing above her. Slap, slap. "Your brother. His car."

This is the first time. Does the woman even have a

brother? This is the first time it is someone she does not know.

"What?" the teacher bristles. "What about my brother?"

"His car. It's burning."

Mrs. Naylor turns a shade of off-white, like old paper. Is she angry? Sick? She drops the ruler on Suzanne's desk and turns, leaving the classroom without a word.

There are one or two giggles from the children, but mostly there is silence. For it is one thing to make fun of Little Sue, another to make fun of her predictions.

Mrs. Naylor is gone for two weeks. There is the hospital time then the funeral, and Mrs. Naylor's replacement in class, Mrs. McCrimmon, stands at the front and does not wander, and never, ever looks Suzanne in the eye. Suzanne notices that others, also, are acting this way now. At the lockers, where there was always much jostling and joking, there is only silence when Suzanne appears. No one pulls Suzanne's hat off and throws it; no one pushes past her to get to his corner.

They have finally realized, they have all finally figured out that Little Sue, Fire Engine Sue, never predicts good things. Oh, there are happy endings— the house fire, Mrs. Reidel's coma—but they are only happy because people arrive in time to intervene.

Why have none of them ever seen this? So greedy were they for the jump on chaos that they saw each intervention as a triumph, their triumph, their mastery.

But Fire Engine Sue speaks chaos.

The next little while is confusing. Adele and Robert Cardinal are called in for meetings with the principal and the school board. Suzanne spends her afternoons reading at home or to Mrs. Reidel. It is nice to have the days again almost like it is summer, but with the cool shiver in the air. She thinks about the penguins. Will she ever be able to build them a shelter? Mrs. Craig at the library laughed at her, right in her face, right beside the SILENCE sign, when she told of her plans.

"Penguins don't live here," said the low voice of the librarian.

Penguins are not seen here now, Suzanne thinks, but that doesn't mean anything. Look at *Mr. Popper's Penguins*, that book Mrs. Reidel gave her. Doesn't prove anything.

Suzanne walks home, a stick in her hand in case any dog wants to play, and she wonders. If she only sees the bad things that could happen, is there someone, some person out there who only sees the good? What would that person be like? Suzanne has tried not to see anything at all, to be like the girls and boys in her class, but when the feeling happens, she can't help it. She wonders why it is that she brings the bad news. Where is the child who walks around lightly, spreading joy?

It is a weary, wary child who makes her way up the driveway to the house, who stands beneath the balcony where her little sister fell. A lock of Carla's hair, a single curl, is in an envelope in her father's desk. Suzanne has seen it twice, the dark swirl resting in its white sleeve.

"Come in, Suzanne." Her mother at the window. "Suppertime."

No homework. No school. Books piled on the table.

"We'll work from home for now," her father says, coughing from the mysterious illness that keeps him at home as well.

"I disturb," she says to the small face in the mirror. She hears the word splash and surface, like a scary catfish, whenever her name is mentioned.

She is visiting a doctor in the city, Doctor Hargreaves. He is a tall man, like her father, with glasses on the tip of his nose. Sometimes he wears them on his head, and his hair eyes stare into the heavens. Or the fluorescent lights. He does not hurt her, and he does not frighten her, he just asks questions about what she does all day, about her pretend games.

"And when you get this feeling...is that what it is, Suzanne, is it a feeling? When you get this feeling, could you tell me what it's like?"

The child shifts on the long leather sofa. Her mother is waiting outside; her father sits in the corner pretending to read. He pretends a lot, just like her.

"It..." What can she say about the blurting urge? "It's a feeling of know—"

"No?"

"Like when you're listening to a story and you think the child will get away or maybe they'll get caught or maybe they'll wake up and it's all a dream and then you know, you just know, they're gonna get caught."

Dr. Hargreaves smiles. "Or maybe they get away." He taps her head with his file folder.

"Yes," Suzanne says, sliding off the couch. "But not when I get the feeling."

There will be further visits. Dr. Hargreaves talks to Suzanne's father, who is nodding.

In the car on the way back, there is not much talking. Suzanne's mother has been to visit Aunt

Sophie, who has passed along a new colouring book and crayons for Suzanne. The child sits in the back seat with the crayons all around her. She has broken one already, the forest-green one, possibly her favourite. She has overworked it, colouring the entire forest both underfoot and overhead, and in the green world, which has only a black-outlined frog in it, she has added a penguin in a penguin house.

I only get the bad news, she tells her doll, Annabelle, at night in bed. *But if I let people know in time, they can maybe stop it. I bring the bad news, but it can still be good.*

•

Her father is reading *Alice in Wonderland* to her. She knows the story by heart. The girl falls down the hole and everything changes. It's just like Carla. Is her father crying as he reads of the girl tumbling head over heels, or is he just happy when she lands safe and sound?

"Papa, it's just a story. Sometimes she goes through mirrors. She does it all the time."

She has seen her father look in a mirror like he could fall through it, press his pale thin face up against the cold, shiny surface and feel it disappear.

"Papa," Suzanne says, her little hand trying to encompass his.

When he cries, it is like a small animal fretting. It is not loud or scary. It's a small sorrow, and Suzanne is not afraid and can hold his hand or, once, his head, and wait. Her Papa comes back, wipes his face and eyes. They have an ice cream cone, if there is any ice cream in the fridge. Or they go to the cold room in the basement and hunt for a bag of secret chocolate raisins.

This father of hers. She asks him, one morning, to put on his suit and tie. She says it's dress-up day and puts on her tunic.

"See? I'm dressed."

He goes into the bedroom and remains there a long time, but when he finally comes out he, too, is dressed. He is wearing the blue-grey suit and the tie Suzanne likes, the one with the dark red diamonds. His shirt is a little wrinkly, but he looks nice.

"Papa, your shoes."

For the plaid slippers do not go with the outfit, despite the dark red in them. He finds his shoes under the living room chair and slowly, laboriously, bends to put them on.

"Beautiful, Papa. You're beautiful."

The man looks down at his daughter, her light brown hair in a ponytail, her tunic neat and collar straight.

"We're all dressed up," he says, "with nowhere to go."

"Let's go see Mommy!"

He has not heard her suggestion.

"Let's go see Mommy at work!"

Most days Robert drives Adele to work, but when he is not well, she takes the bus that gets her close to the office. The town is not big, but the company she works for is on the very edge of town in the new business park. Suzanne climbs into the back seat. She finds a crayon that was lost and props it up in the car-door ashtray so she won't forget it.

"Mommy will sure be surprised," she says, but the man in the front seat hears her. His blue-grey shoulders go up and down, he sighs once, and starts the engine.

From the back seat, with her feet up, Suzanne watches the town go by sideways. Mrs. Reidel's house cruises into view. Her trees are fighting with the wind. Soon it will snow, and they will rest.

"Will I go back to school?" she asks suddenly, as if it has just occurred to her that she might not.

Her father jerks his head to the right to let her know he is listening.

"Yes…of course you'll go. But, listen, maybe…maybe we can make a little deal. Like, a secret between us, you know?"

"Oh, yes!" Suzanne inclines her face toward the secret as her father pulls into the parking lot of her mother's building. He turns the engine off and swings around to face her.

"How about when you go back, you don't tell people when you get a special feeling, okay? It will be our secret, just you and me and no one else. What do you think, Little Sue?"

Suzanne flips the thought over in her mind. It is not like she has any particular choice when it happens. Could she keep such a feeling inside? Would it hurt?

They walk into the reception area and take the stairs up to the second floor. Suzanne knows her mother's desk. It is near the window, and she has a leaf plant there, drinking the sunlight.

But she is not at her desk. Suzanne recognizes the rock she has painted and given to her mother as a paperweight. It is sitting on the desk, and it is working; it is weighing down a bunch of papers that would otherwise fly away. Suzanne's father is talking to the lady her mother works with, who is telling them that

Mrs. Cardinal has gone out to lunch.

"It's early for lunch," Robert Cardinal observes, wondering whether or not to go home.

The woman tries not to stare, but she is studying the man they have all heard about, who stays home all day while his wife goes out to work, stays home with his child who, herself, does not go to school. The father of the child who died.

"Will she be back soon?" he asks.

The woman is vague about *soon,* about people being sick of the little restaurant in the business park.

"Please don't tell her, then, that we were here. It was a surprise. The child's surprise."

They re-button their coats, and her Papa puts her hat on back to front. He holds his head up as they walk to the stairwell, as their steps echo on the way down.

They are getting in the car, they are in the car, in fact, when Suzanne sees a dark blue automobile pull into the space on the other side of the lot. The door slices open, and a man unfolds who might be Mommy's boss but without the glasses. Then the other door.

"There! There's Mommy! C'mon, Papa."

She would have been out the door, but for the hand blocking the lock button.

"No...no," her father whispers. "This will just be a secret, okay? Just a secret."

He wrenches himself around and adjusts the rearview mirror, and Suzanne can see him holding the secret in. He is in pain, her Papa, but he is clamping it all in. Her Papa can do it. Maybe she can, too. The drive home is quiet, which gives her time to think.

Little Sue can keep secrets. She kept the one about the

broken trophy at the back of the classroom, the result of a ball thrown by Alan Conway. In a way, Suzanne and her father are like spies, two secret agents on missions to save the world. Robert Cardinal and Fire Engine Sue.

•

In the winter, the path beside the river is filled up with snow, but Suzanne can get partway down, as far as the little clearing where she would like to build her penguin house.

Penguins like snow. It's normal for them, like her beanbag chair is normal for her. She works hard and alone, packing snow, building up ridges. There will be levels, like steps, for them to come and go. She loves the way their wings flap just a little. The ones she saw at the zoo with Auntie Sophie flapped their wings a bit and did not so much fly as waddle over to the next rock. She could do that. Anyone could. She likes penguins, because they are not show-offs.

"A frozen home for you, like living in a popsicle."

It would be too cold for her. Already her parents have warned her about the terribly cold temperatures this winter. She doesn't feel it, except in her fingers and toes. They get wet and stay wet the entire afternoon. One more little flat part to make, and the first part of the penguin house will be finished. Wind whips around her ears, and she pulls her toque lower. She lies sideways in the snow, eyeing the level of the platform. It looks good. Even. Penguins could dance.

It is silent like this. Her left ear, pressed to the

ground and muffled by the snow, hears nothing. Her right hears only the whisper of the wind. She lies there for a while, watching the snow "V" made by her mitten. It's so quiet. The voices of her parents fade, the tears and the choked up words at night, like the song she liked that wouldn't come in on the car radio, her parents' voices and the car radio, fading in and out and getting buried when they drove through the tunnel.

She is cold, then not so cold. She is thinking of resting before heading back onto the windy pathway. She is supposed to stop at Mrs. Reidel's to see if she needs anything, but she has worked hard, and she deserves a rest, just a short one. She lies in the snow waiting for the penguins to arrive.

When the feeling comes, she almost doesn't know it. When it comes, she is comfortable and sleepy, and she feels nothing much, just weary and so cozy. The feeling works harder, pushing at the edges, jabbing at her with needle spikes.

"Ow..." she murmurs softly. Tiny shifting left and right.

Jab.

"Ow!"

She wants to sleep, just sleep. And then a girl is sleeping, too, and everybody's crying. Her mother in a veil, her father's knuckles white. There are flower smells, lilies and roses and those yellow things Mrs. Reidel grows.

And she must get up. She must push up from the soft world. White lights are burning into her, long corridors of light lead her forward, stumbling, incandescence of short candles, toward a village in the distance. Penguins. And home.

A girl in a blue cloth jacket and a red toque is found in a clearing by the river path. She is carrying no identification and is taken to the local clinic where Nurse Carter recognizes Suzanne and calls her parents.

Little Sue, Fire Engine Sue, is going to the hospital in the next town, where the doctors will take her temperature, which everyone is watching like the stock market, and will take the baby finger on her right hand.

There will be consultation and wailing, but when Suzanne returns home, she will have one finger less to count on.

Cards arrive from the school, her mother's work and a few of the children Suzanne knows. The church sends over fruit and a Bible, and Mrs. Reidel has Florence, her part-time helper, bring over a stuffed animal. It is only when Suzanne sees the squat funny penguin that she realizes Mrs. Reidel knows. She knows what happened in the clearing. What good is a gift if you can't use it now and then, she'd say. She'd open the tin of biscuits, and they would munch conspiratorially, and the afternoon would slide like snow from the roof of a car.

.

In spring, when Suzanne is back at school ("no more strange feelings, not for a long time"), something happens in the town. Mr. Laturelle's son, Frank, who has been away so long that Suzanne doesn't remember him, returns. But not alone. No. He arrives with shoulder-length, matted hair, a beard and a girlfriend named Holly.

Holly is a hippie. That's what Mrs. Craig at the

library said. Holly has long, straight hair with a braid at either side of her face. She wears long cotton dresses with flowers and squiggles on them and sometimes a coat that is shorter than the dress or, when it is warmer, a shawl almost the same as Mrs. Reidel's. Her glasses, too, are like Mrs. Reidel's, round metal frames that sit on her nose or the top of her head.

Suzanne has seen her precisely three times so far, but Holly has fascinated her each time. The first time, it was still snowy out, and Holly was wearing old boots and the too-short coat. She was coming out of the IGA, and Suzanne was going in with her parents. Her mother moved aside completely to let Holly pass. As she did, the hippie girl looked right at Suzanne and said, "Can't wait till we can wear sandals, eh?"

Which seemed like such a sensible thing to say that Suzanne replied, "Yeah, and shorts, too," before feeling her arm yanked.

Suzanne has seen her on two other occasions, and the woman always seems to notice her.

And now Suzanne hears that Holly and Frank are going to have a baby. A baby! She didn't even know they were married. And now it is Mrs. Craig's voice that is rising in the library as she goes on about hell and handbaskets. She almost thumps the book on Suzanne's missing finger.

"Oh…sorry, Little Sue. You go home now. It's not safe for kids to be out on the street any more."

Suzanne hasn't seen Holly for a while. Frank is working in his father's store, his hair in a ponytail and his beard shorter and less scraggly. She could ask Frank. The shop is on her way home, so it is no trouble

31

to stamp her rainboots on the mat outside and open the door into this world of penny candy, fly-paper and sewing machine oil.

Frank is bringing a box out from the back of the store. He plops it down on the counter and brushes a wisp of wayward hair from his eyes. "Good afternoon, Ma'am. What can I do for you?"

She smiles. She isn't Ma'am. Her mother is Ma'am.

"I have a fine collection of penny candy here, for the most discerning of buyers. Feast your eyes on the mountain of jujubes, and over there, the world's largest jar of jellybeans. Really. It's been documented. Or perhaps your taste runs to the more exotic?" He leaps over the counter like an excited rodent.

"Anise-seed balls. Anise from the far reaches of the earth, specially grown and harvested. Balls from the centre of the earth, harnessed at great peril by intrepid ball-collectors."

She is staring at Frank.

He stops. "Okay, so what is it? I'm trying to keep from going crazy here."

"How could you go crazy in here. There's so *much!*"

He casts his glance around and lets it rest on the floor mops in the corner.

"Yeah," he says with a nod. "You're right."

"How is Holly? That's why I came."

Frank comes around from the counter and crouches beside her.

"Do you know something? You're the first person who's asked. The very first. My lady is fine, if you can call throwing up in the toilet all morning fine."

"Throwing up."

"It's a having-baby thing. She's okay, just a little tired. She's resting more these days."

"Because I haven't seen her."

"Yeah. Like I say. How do you know Holly?"

"We…uh…we…talk a little."

"Well, I'd be happy to tell her you asked. What's your name?"

"Oh, she doesn't know…it's Suzanne. Sue. Fire Engine Sue." She pops her mouth shut. Why has that come out?

Frank steps back to look at her. "You're Fire Engine Sue? I've been wanting to meet you. I didn't realize you were so young. You're the girl who predicted the broken leg outside the store."

Suzanne closes her eyes. "I'm sorry. Your father…it's just that…I'm not supposed to talk about it."

"I've heard other things as well. I'm very happy to know you, Suzanne. And I'm sure my lady will be pleased you asked after her. Maybe you can come around and visit her sometime."

Suzanne nods and shifts a little toward the door. "I…gotta go."

"Right. Hey, wait!"

He leaps over the counter again and digs beneath it, retrieving a large peppermint stick. "A gift. No charge."

"I'm not…"

"Allowed? Hey, maybe it is a little on the ostentatious side, candy-wise. Plus, it's hard to hide. How 'bout a gum ball? You should see where the ball collectors travel to find those. Rubber trees in the rainforest…"

He is about to go off on a story again, so she selects one.

"White. Nobody picks white."

She smiles at him. "Doesn't stain your mouth," she says before dropping it in.

●

A few days later, Suzanne knocks at the door. She is carrying a crêpe and pipe-cleaner flower she has made in class. It is red, and she has sprayed some of her mother's Shalimar on it, so it smells. She knocks again. This time she hears thumpy footsteps. The apartment is above the hardware store, and she has never been there before.

Creeaaakkkk. Funny that the hardware door creaks.

"Hello," she says, holding out the drooping flower.

The woman is Holly, only she looks tired and stretched out like a rag on Mrs. Reidel's clothesline. Her hair looks like strings.

"Hi there. Frank said you were visiting. Come in, come in. Is this for me?"

Suzanne nods. "I made it in school."

"It's…lovely…I…" And Holly sneezes an elaborate sneeze worthy of Suzanne's father.

"I put perfume in it."

Holly nods and carries the flower down the hall. "Take your coat off," she calls. When she returns, she has a tray in her hands.

"Sit down. Take the load off."

Suzanne does as she is told and sits neatly on the edge of a bench along the wall. It looks like it could have come out of a church. She runs her hand along the edge.

"Yes, neat, eh? We found it in a field."

Suzanne tucks her hands in her lap as she has seen

people do on TV. She notices that she always tucks the missing finger underneath, the place where the real finger would be.

"Juice? It's really good. Mango and orange and, I think, some other tropical fruit."

Suzanne only knows orange, but she agrees to a glass. There are lumpy cookies on a plate that Holly passes her. They are huge and a little strange, and she is about to decline when Holly adds, "I made these myself." So Suzanne selects the closest one, as she has been taught, and holds it cautiously.

"Frank said you were asking about me."

"Yes," she almost whispers. "I didn't see you for a long time."

"No, well, did he tell you why? That I'm going to have a baby?" She smiles and for a second looks like the Holly who had come to town.

"I didn't know people could have babies if they weren't married."

"Oh, people can do a lot of things without getting married."

"Don't you want to? Get married?"

The woman stands up, her hand on her stomach, and paces the small room. "No. I mean, you don't need to. Frank and I love each other. I mean, there are people out there who tell you things, but they don't know. People who try to run your life, you know?"

Suzanne nods, turning over her cookie.

"Sesame seeds, if you're wondering. And sunflower."

Seeds like the birdseeds in Mrs. Reidel's feeder.

"Do people ever try to run your life? I'm sorry...what should I call you, Suzanne?"

The girl shrugs. "People call me lots of things…too."

"I've heard names. Why do they call you those things, Suzanne?"

"They don't mean anything. Even Mrs. Reidel calls me Little Sue sometimes. It's just a name."

"And Fire Engine Sue? That's just a name as well?"

Suzanne shifts uncomfortably. This is getting near the edges of her secret. She promised Papa. "People say stuff 'cause they don't know me. What are you going to call your baby?'"

The cookie is tastier than she thought it would be, the raisins soft.

"Names?" Holly laughs. "We haven't talked about it yet. The baby is only about this big right now."

She holds her fingers apart to reveal an alarmingly miniature imaginary baby. Suzanne blinks. Baby always means Carla, Carla in her crib while the home fills up with smoke. This is hardly real. How can Holly believe it?

"How do you know?" Suzanne reaches for another cookie.

"Well, that's how long it takes. I won't have the baby for months and months, and it will be growing all along, and then I'll be this big." She holds out her arms around a huge air stomach. "Did you ever see a pregnant woman? Really big?"

Suzanne gulps down a chunk of cookie. She can almost remember her mother tottering around with a tummy balloon, a green top covering it like a grassy hill. Her mother lying on her side, and the hill so green and safe. Carla.

Suzanne visits Holly often over that season, pressing

her hands up against the growing baby through the filmy Indian cotton shirt. Sometimes Holly is resting when she arrives (Frank has given the child a key), and she sets about dusting or tidying up the cramped apartment. Once she finds a striped baby set—pants, top and a little bonnet. She wonders whether Holly found it in the city, or whether someone sent it as a gift. She hopes it is a gift.

Time goes slowly, then more quickly. School ends. Suzanne is once more free, and she can visit both Mrs. Reidel and Holly on the same day. The houses dress for summer, with hanging plants, trimmed hedges and bird feeders. There are sprinklers on many front lawns. A person can stay entirely wet all summer if they know where to go. On Suzanne's own property, a spitting sprinkler sprays a semi-circle of grass. No one turns it to water the other half. No one seems to notice or care. The lawn responds with a rich green crescent that is kind of like a filled-in fairy ring.

Robert Cardinal's summer allergies have worsened; his eyes are always red, and his nose runs. He sits indoors at the kitchen table doing crossword puzzles or playing solitaire. Sometimes he reads the paper. In the evenings he might take a walk, and his daughter goes along with him.

He never speaks to her about the secret, his or hers. They are two spies, tight-lipped, too clever by far to risk untold danger by opening their big mouths. So they stroll along, listening to the peepers and the bullfrogs, the man listening only to the noise, and the child to the song. One evening, fireflies. One evening, june bugs, attracted to the street lights, their bodies clicking on the pavement as they fall. He points above him and tells her of planetary dust, of polestars and the naming of stars. And he says, "I don't know if your mother will go away."

The words hang there, like fireflies flashing. It is dark, but she sees his face every time they pass under a street light. He has a long, thin face, her Papa. Longer and thinner than ever.

"She might. She might go. I don't know," he says.

The bugs crawl to the light, flitting their wings. Suzanne puts her hand into the clammy hand of her father, and they walk as far as the deserted ballpark before turning back toward the house.

•

Adele Cardinal does not go away, though observers might debate this, for she works late three nights a week and is distracted when she is at home. When Suzanne tells her a story about a river and a canoe, she stares right through the girl as though the river and the canoe and even Suzanne do not exist. When Robert Cardinal holds the chair for her at supper, she doesn't even acknowledge the chair, let alone the gesture.

They are three people with their secrets. It is like the TV show, like the Cone of Silence on *Get Smart*, where the Chief can't hear what Agent 86 is saying. Aunt Sophie calls in the evenings, and Adele goes into the bedroom with the phone, the extension cord stretched so tight around the door that there are no more coils in it.

One evening when they are home, the feeling comes again. Suzanne is playing with her horses: all five plastic horses are in this game, and the kleenex box corral is on her bed, so she is fenced in. This makes her laugh, because it is just like that song she heard, and she sings "Don't Fence Me In" as she puts up her makeshift barriers. She doesn't know what all the words mean: cottonwood, though it is supposed to be some kind of tree; cayuse, no idea. She wonders about the Western Sky, and whether it is the only place you can wander over yonder.

And then it is upon her. She is not allowed out at night except with a parent, and she has promised and promised. She looks at the horses. Her baby doll pyjamas are too lightweight, so she pulls her pedal-pushers over them and throws on her squall jacket. Her window is next to the tree. She has done this before, though never at night.

Lifting the window sash, she edges across the frame and feels with her foot for the crook in the tree. Yes. The rest is a blur as she pushes off into the tree and wriggles down the trunk. She's cut her leg; she can feel it. Dropping to the ground, she is already running, racing along, sockless in her sneakers, past Mrs. Reidel's house, past the IGA, to the apartment on top of the hardware store.

She bangs at the door, trying to catch her breath, bent over from the exertion. The door opens slowly, and Frank's bushy head peers around.

"What the...what are you doing here, Suzanne?" He holds the door wide for her, and she tumbles in. "You're a pleasure always, but I have to say this is a little inconvenient. Holly is asleep, and I was just about to head off myself... Hey, what's wrong?"

Suzanne speaks slowly, fighting the words every step of the way.

"Holly's got to go to the hospital."

Frank pulls a cigarette paper from the packet. "What, now?"

"When…when she has the baby. She has to be in the hospital."

Frank shakes his head. "You know how she feels. She wants to have this baby naturally. None of that pumped-up crap for her. She's a natural woman, and she…"

"Frank!"

Frank stops. The little girl is crying. She is frantic. She is Fire Engine Sue.

"Why? Can you tell me that? Why, Suzanne?"

"She's gonna need a doctor."

"The baby…Christ… Tell me what you mean!"

He grabs her as if to shake her but just holds her as she says, "The baby will need the doctor."

They sit together on the paisley couch. Frank's eyes are filling, and Suzanne's are how dry. She sits with Frank for a while. He drives her back home in his Volkswagen, leaving her three houses away, at her request.

Because Frank cried, she knows he believed her. Holly will be okay, Suzanne tells herself, pulling up the tree hand over hand.

She sits on her bed, the horses haphazard on the floor. One horse is in her hand, and she sucks on the plastic fetlock. She broke her word to her father.

Broken promises or lies.

Or a little baby dies.

•

They take her to the midway, a place she has never

asked to go. They also bring along Annie Fournier, a new-ish girl from one street over whose mother works at the same company as Suzanne's mother. Both are only children. Neither likes the midway.

"It'll be fun, that's why," Adele explains.

Her daughter's silence somehow infuriates.

"You need to get out more. She's the same age as you are. And it's the midway! When I was your age, I couldn't wait for it to come to town!"

Suzanne puts on her blue jeans and the bright flowered top that is getting too small, removes it, and pulls on an oversized T-shirt.

Annie Fournier arrives with a plastic bag in tow. She doesn't exactly scowl at Suzanne, but she makes it wordlessly clear that this is not her idea either. The girls sit side by side in the living room while Mrs. Cardinal bustles in the kitchen, putting things in her carry-all.

Suzanne's father is outside at the car, throwing Suzanne's candy bar wrappers into a small bucket he keeps handy but never handy enough. Soon they are off, and the dreaded silence fills the back seat where the two child islands float. When Robert Cardinal turns a corner, the islands bump, lightly, but otherwise remain two distinct land masses.

"Well, come on, girls! What's your favourite ride, Annie? Which one are you really looking forward to?" Mr. Cardinal glances back.

It turns out Annie Fournier likes the midway. It is just Suzanne she does not like.

"Maybe the Wild Mouse. Do you think they'll have a Salt and Pepper this year?"

Mr. Cardinal signals out the window. "Wouldn't know.

Kind of a big contraption. We haven't gone to the midway in a long time, so you probably know more about it than we do. When was the last time we went, Adele?"

Mrs. Cardinal jerks out of her thoughts and shakes her head. "Long time. Suzanne was only five or so. The year of the fire, I think."

Suzanne is stunned. "I been there before?"

She remembers nothing at all of midways, rides. They must be mistaken. "What rides did I like?"

Mrs. Cardinal shakes her head. "Oh, you were too young and too small for any of the big rides, but you did like the kiddie-world merry-go-round, and the little boats, and you and Carla…"

Oh dear. Oh dear, oh dear.

Silence in the front seat now, as Robert pulls into the makeshift parking lot. Annie Fournier jabs a fingernail into Suzanne's right arm and whispers, "Too scared for any of the real rides. Big surprise. Maybe you can go on the little boats again."

Suzanne follows the procession onto the grounds of the midway.

•

This Annie Fournier is not an evil girl. Suzanne cannot say she is evil. But she is a girl with plans. A crafty girl, as Mrs. Reidel might say. She has already wrapped her hand around the arm of Mr. Cardinal for the walk over to the hot dog stand, and now she is attempting to insinuate herself into Mrs. Cardinal's good graces. Hah. Mrs. Cardinal is not going to hold her hand, or rub her back when she is scared. Still, the new girl is beaming up at Mrs. Cardinal and is getting a smile back that Suzanne only remembers.

The hot dogs are cold. There is a bug in the relish.

"What's wrong with you? Eat up! We only have another hour to go on the rides!"

Mr. Cardinal is buoyant, cleaning up his hot dog and chasing Annie Fournier around to grab handfuls of her cotton candy.

"Oh, Robert, get your own," Mrs. Cardinal laughs. Laughs!

"You done?" Adele scoops up Suzanne's hot dog and wipes the girl's mouth with a paper serviette. Then it is back on the rides. The Wild Mouse is next, and Annie has convinced the Cardinals to put Suzanne on it with her. Her eyes glow in the reflection of the flaking bulbs that line the path to the ride. Suzanne is bolted in beside Annie. The ride commences. Suzanne's head is forced back like a giant invisible hand pressing her forehead. Round and back, this way and that, slammed forward, thrust back. Annie Fournier's head is the same as hers, forward and back. Noise. Lights. It is too much, too…

When she vomits, she decorates the car, but mostly she decorates Annie Fournier. Suzanne sees a shriek frozen on Annie's face. Anger, incredulity. When the ride stops, the attendant grunts at the girls to get out. Annie Fournier spills off the ride and runs to the exit screaming and crying. Mrs. Cardinal takes her hand and tries to wipe her shirt before moving away with her. Suzanne staggers to the exit as the attendant hoses down the car. Her father is there waiting for her.

"Sorry, Papa," she murmurs, not trusting herself to open her mouth.

Her father steers her head toward the car. "Didn't know your aim was that good," he says.

·

She hears no more of Annie Fournier for a while. But one day Mrs. Cardinal comes home from work with the idea that it would be lovely if Annie Fournier came over once a week to play.

"With you?" Suzanne asks.

"No, with you."

Why do they do this? Why can't they leave her alone? Suzanne looks around her bedroom, determined to hide anything of real value. Her rocks, her doll, Annabelle, the key chain with the rubber dog, the horses with the chewed fetlocks. No way will Annie Fournier get her treasures.

Summer spins into fall, and Annie Fournier's visits continue. On the other side of town, at the James Street Hospital, Holly gives birth to a healthy boy. People in town are ambivalent. While they don't approve of her non-wedded state, they certainly wish her and the child no ill.

They reserve most of their disdain for Frank, who carries the baby around like he owns it.

Frank and Holly and the baby find Suzanne on the way to the library. Holly is pushing the baby in an old pram that squeaks. Frank is making faces into the pram.

"Suzanne! We were looking for you the last few days! We didn't want to go by your house," Frank added. Nod and a wink.

"He wanted to thank you," Holly says, coming

round to kiss and hug Suzanne.

"I did have complications. If I hadn't been in hospital...well...thank you so much."

Suzanne looks into the pram. Tiny-fingered child, eyes and fists clenched tight. Dark wisps of hair, and the red and white toque in this chill air.

"His name is Maurice Falcon, but we're going to call him Falcon."

Falcon.

"Keen of eye, strong of flight," says Frank.

"I like his name," Suzanne says. "Just don't call him Little Falcon."

"Or Fire Engine Falcon, right? Whoa! That has a ring to it, though."

"You'll come and visit sometime?"

Suzanne nods. "I hope so," she smiles at the happy family.

•

She does not get any feelings and does not know that by Christmas, Frank will have left town for greener pastures.

•

Too bad Annie Fournier wouldn't just disappear. Fold up and get tucked away somewhere like the registration sheet for Brownies that her mother lost that fall.

They are in Suzanne's room. Annie Fournier has appropriated Suzanne's Barbie doll. She is amazed that Suzanne has only one.

"Me, I have six, almost."

Suzanne does not want to know about the "almost" doll. Truth is Suzanne has not figured out the hard-bodied dolls, so different from Annabelle, and so unresponsive compared to the frogs by the river. Annie Fournier can have the doll if she wants it. Maybe she'll leave the other stuff alone.

"How come you have so many Barbies? How come your mother buys you so many?"

Annie snorts. "She's not my mother! I got no mother. I just live there 'cause they tell me to."

This is news.

Annie Fournier, whose mother works with Mrs. Cardinal, *has* no mother?

"She fosters. She's no mother to me."

This is a world Suzanne does not know at all, a world of no mothers or fathers, where children travel across town or between towns to live with people who are not their parents. She doesn't know what to say to Annie Fournier.

"Are you sad? That you have no parents?"

Annie Fournier is edging a Barbie earring into the plastic smiling head.

"Doesn't matter. She gives me all the Barbies, right?"

They sit in unaccustomed silence.

No mother or father. Suzanne can't understand it. When Carla was gone, it was so strange, like one part of the house disappearing, like you'd walk down the hall to go into a room, but the room wasn't there any more. You opened the door into a blank. No parents? Like there was no house at all.

•

In the weeks leading up to Christmas, Suzanne knows something is going on. Her parents are actually excited about the season again, decorating the house with the vinyl wreath, the fake poinsettias. They're going to get a real Christmas tree after a couple of years of artificial. Her father, despite his terrible health, has spent all of one Saturday putting up lights outside. The porch roof, the banister. He comes back inside red-faced and not coughing. Suzanne watches carefully as she gums a social tea biscuit.

And then they tell her. It is all arranged. Annie Fournier will not be coming over once a week to play with her. Annie Fournier will be moving in, living with the Cardinals, sharing Suzanne's room!

Suzanne sits back in the armchair.

"There's no…but there's no room…in my room…" she sputters.

They can't mean this. She's had no feeling, no warning.

"It's the same size it was. You would have shared it, eventually, with Carla."

The name so plainly spoken. Carla slipping down under the earth.

Two weeks later, and three days before Christmas, Annie Fournier arrives. She takes the side of the room without the window as a gesture of cooperation, or perhaps because it's bigger, and sticks her meagre collection of pocket books on the shelf beside Suzanne's. Her Barbies have been brought in a bag, and Suzanne has been persuaded by her mother to donate her large blue plastic storage box to Annie as a home for the dolls.

The girls sit in front of the tree. Is Suzanne seeing things, or have Carla's ornaments reappeared on the branches? Her father is smiling as he pokes at the fire in the fireplace. Her mother enters the room with a tray of little punch glasses of eggnog. Everyone gathers round and takes a glass. Her father raises his.

"Merry Christmas, girls."

They click.

That night in bed, waiting for Christmas to come, Suzanne listens to Annie's kid-snores. After her bath, Suzanne had felt her mother tug the arm of her bathrobe on her way down the hall. She turned, and her mother gave her a long hug.

"You'll never be alone again," she whispered into the damp hair.

Now, peering through the crack between the curtain and the window's edge, listening to Annie Fournier turn over in her bed, Suzanne blinks back tears.

Goodbye, Carla.

In the blue-black night.

Merry Christmas, girls.

All of it, all of this, so they could say those words again.

•

Annie Fournier is a bigger girl than Suzanne, so when the Cardinals buy two of anything, Annie has the bigger size. This starts out innocently enough, but soon the pattern develops. When things are too small for Annie, they go to Suzanne. Suzanne's blue pants and matching top outfit is too small but, luckily, Annie's old red one fits her now.

"I don't like red," Suzanne protests.
"Nonsense," her mother replies.
"Fire Engine Sue," Annie chants.

•

It sounds horrible, life in the Cardinal family. But
mostly it is a question of territory. Suzanne keeps away
from Annie as much as she can, while Annie explores
the newfound joy of having a home. No one in town
can deny her this joy. After all, the kid has been
bounced from place to place for a number of years.
Who can blame her if she is a little proprietary? Mr.
and Mrs. Cardinal can see that the child is starved for
attention, and besides, there is no point in taking on
the job if you do not intend to do it properly.

It is too bad about the other child, Little Sue. Too
bad she hasn't adjusted more successfully to the new
situation. One would think that another sister...a
sister again. But one never knew with kids, and that
one was strange from the word go. People in town
know what a handful she is. There is actually some
renewed sympathy for Adele and Robert Cardinal, a
goodwill not seen since the death of Carla and certainly
not during Adele's affair with her boss. As for Robert,
well, he was a hopeless case for a long time, but lately
he's actually been tolerably friendly, patting Jim Harlow
on the back at the hardware store and laughing at one
of Wilson Craig's lame jokes. Everyone in town agrees
that, on balance, the adopted kid is a good idea.

Suzanne taps on Mrs. Reidel's porch window. She
can see the old woman in there, dozing in her big

armchair. Her wheelchair is close by, with Ferg curled up on it. Suzanne raps harder on the window, and Mrs. Reidel stirs. Suzanne thinks she is recognized through the curtain, because she is waved to the door. Suzanne nods and retrieves the key from behind the porch broom. Everyone knows where Mrs. Reidel keeps her key.

Suzanne opens the door. Very warm inside to combat Mrs. Reidel's recent chills. Suzanne removes her boots and coat and rubs her hands together before hurrying into the front room to sit with her friend. Lately the old woman wants to be read to, fairy tales or funny stuff, so Suzanne brings over her childhood books. They have read "The Poor Little Match Girl" and "The Little Fir Tree". Suzanne doesn't want to read "Rose Red and Rose White".

"Sisters," says Mrs. Reidel. Suzanne nods.

They have just finished their old favourite, *The Snow Queen*, and Suzanne cries, as she always does when Kay cannot recognize Gerda. Gerda has travelled all the way to Finland to find him. She even gives away her boots and walks barefoot through the icy cold. She finds him in the palace of the Snow Queen, and he does not know her.

Mrs. Reidel puts an arm around Suzanne's shoulder. It is the bad arm from the stroke, and it barely touches, but Suzanne can feel it.

"I know who you are," the old woman whispers. "Never you fear."

It is not long after this visit that Mrs. Reidel dies. Suzanne is in school when her mother arrives at the classroom door. Afterward, Suzanne will marvel at her mother's gesture, this admission of so much, but the moment it happens, all she feels is a dull confusion as she is shuffled out into the hall and home.

"I didn't want you to hear it on the way home," her mother explains.

There is nothing to do but sit in her half-bedroom and cry. Annie Fournier will be home in a couple of hours. Until then, it is Suzanne's room, and she sits by the window watching the tree branches move.

Many people attend Mrs. Reidel's funeral. Her son has arrived, looking strange with his moustache and his lumpy suit. People haven't seen Albert in a dog's age. He's put on weight. He looks the worse for wear. That's what happens to people who don't visit their mothers.

Frank Laturelle is there, without Holly and Falcon. He has actually come back for the funeral because Mrs. Reidel used to babysit him when he was a kid. Suzanne listens to all this news. Mrs. Reidel was a great beauty. More news. Suzanne has loved every wrinkle in the old woman's face, and she has seen one faded photograph of a young and hearty woman at the guardrail of a boat, but a beauty?

"Could have had any man in town back then."

But how large is the town?

"She was a cracker. She could have gone to the city and married rich. But she gave it all up to marry old Reidel, there."

Charlie Reidel. Died in the Fifties and left her the house and some bonds and little else. Albert, the son, moved into the city, and the old woman was left to pine away, all those years, alone.

"Shame," people say, as the hearse pulls up to the church.

Suzanne sits in a pew on her own, near the front. She makes the Sign of the Cross with her head down, studying the kneeler. The service is long, and Suzanne wonders about the painted swirling trim at the top of the altar. That would be a hard job. Tricky.

Albert the son is doing a reading. He stumbles over words, and anyone can see he is crying. Suzanne thinks of Mrs. Reidel's sour, minty breath right beside her, whispering to her, "I know who you are."

Never you fear.

Children of the Revolution

1973

You wedge the book in behind the centre drawer of the olive-coloured desk. You have discovered this secret space—the miscalculation of a carpenter?—and seized it, silently. Yours. This space. The book is a discarded agenda from the real estate company that employs your father. Real estate! Robert Cardinal, who used to run in circles in the basement, is now a real estate agent. The agenda is old, from 1971, but you have torn out the few used pages and made it, like the crevice behind the drawer, your own. Over the embossed Oakstand Realties logo, you have glued pieces of material, a collage of paisley and madras that you hope looks exotic. Over the gold-stamped 1971 you have pasted a satin label on which you have written: *My Book of Me, 1973.*

Of course you hide it. Annie Fournier is everywhere. Her schoolbooks trail down the hall. Her bra is slung over the chair beside her bed. Annie Fournier, only a year and a half older than you, has budded, blossomed and bloomed. She wears her school uniform as if it is a Halloween costume, rolling the grey skirt up around the waist band, until it is a mini, then squeezing into her white blouse or the turtleneck she favours. You, on the other hand, are gamine, elfin. A slightly wild look appears on your face, at least it does when you look in the mirror.

At the bus stop, Annie Fournier stands with a clump of girls who, like her, are too big for their clothes. They laugh, one even smokes, and they look years older than fourteen and fifteen.

One day when you are standing near them you hear the tall one, her hair lightened with Lemon-Up, say, "I can't believe you're sisters." You are studying a broken Coke bottle when you hear Annie Fournier reply, "Yeah. She's adopted."

Of course you hide the book. Not that there is anything so earth-shattering in it. You need to have a life to have a journal, your mother told you when you asked for a diary for Christmas. So, the agenda, which was on its way to the trash when you rescued it. You look over the first page.

My Book of Me, 1973.

WHAT I LOST:
A sister
Part of a finger
WHAT I GAINED:
Part of a sister
I am thirteen.

WHAT I OWN:
This book.

You shimmy out the long green drawer, pressing the book in before sliding the drawer back into place. Annie Fournier bursts into the room and flops on her bed.

"What are you looking at?" she demands.

You turn back to the novel at your bedside. You have been in it for weeks now and are crawling your way through the Shire with Frodo. You don't know why you took it from the shelf in the school library. It is huge, and there are three parts to it. But you noticed someone reading it on a bus once and, more importantly, you remember seeing it at Holly's place before Holly moved away.

After Frank left, Holly stayed on a while with Baby Falcon. But Holly told you that she couldn't stand Frank's father nosing around all the time. So Holly and Falcon went to the bus station one morning, and you haven't seen them since. Falcon would be big now, like the kids in the sandlot at the park. The Beatles were singing "All You Need Is Love" back then, and you think that Holly must have believed it.

> *You could have asked me.*
> *WHAT I KNOW:*
> *People might like you, but maybe for the wrong reasons.*
> *People have respect for somebody that doesn't panic.*

In the high school cafeteria, you are dwarfed by the older kids. You focus on a spot on the back wall and move like a rodent toward it. This gets you through the maze of orange plastic chairs. You are convinced that people will think you have a friend back there and are making your way to a destination.

Like Frodo.

Today as you get to the far wall, you find yourself standing next to a thin, gangly boy. He is older. He must be in grade ten or eleven. He is standing at the wall as if he, too, is waiting for a mysterious friend to arrive, to invite him to sit down. He stares at you then turns away.

...he knows me.

You feel a slight hiccup in your heart.

Meanwhile, there are Black Riders all around you and you would make yourself invisible if you could.

Frodo has a secret.

Just like me.

How long has it been since you've had an episode? That is what the doctor has decided to call your feeling.

Like on TV. Episode Five—see a kid fall down an escalator.

You remember the feeling, the flushed, feverish face, your heart thumping erratically, how you were tongue-tied yet gasping to speak.

It's like being in love, maybe.

At night in your half of the bedroom, you try to fall asleep. Annie Fournier has had a long day—practice at lunch and handball after school. She snores deliciously, savouring the air on both sides of the transparent wall you've erected. Mrs. Reidel had had an imaginary wall with her cat Ferg, but Ferg always ended up sleeping on her bed.

WHAT I WANT TO KNOW:
-How to write on paperyrus.
-How to spell paperyrus.
-About snoring.
-Who is the boy in the cafeteria?

Your visits to the doctor are infrequent now. Mrs. Cardinal swears it was a phase and is over. Mr. Cardinal agrees with her but always gives you a sideways glance as she says it. Both parents think it is Annie Fournier, the addition of Annie Fournier, that has saved you.

"Loneliness can make strange things happen," Adele Cardinal says in the kitchen one night.

You aren't listening at the door; you haven't done that in ages. But you overhear it, and your father's response. "Is there anything you want to tell me?"

There are pot noises and the sound of steel wool scrubbing, but there is also a silence that reaches around the door and right back to the living room.

Love
(I would like to know about)

Annie Fournier's handball team has won the local championship. They will be going to the regionals. Everyone at school is ecstatic. Annie walks with the team now, her bus stop friends forgotten. These girls don't need to wear their jerseys in the halls; they are immediately recognizable. It's the way they walk— deliberate, cocky—daring people to interfere.

You stay out of their way. You tread the line between classrooms with a practiced agility, dodging open lockers and couples hand in hand. You do this, amazingly, with your head down, and most of the time you are successful.

On one particular afternoon, it is your downcast eyes that are the cause of a collision. You bang into the obstruction before you know it and, upon raising your eyes, see the boy from the cafeteria. He wears the school uniform of grey pants and white shirt, but his pants are strange; they look almost woven. There is no fly. Why are you looking there? The shirt has no buttons and has apparently been made on his body. He could have stepped out of another time, except for the hint of a psychedelic T-shirt peeking out from beneath the uniform.

"Oh, sorry," you begin, but before either of you can say another word, the barging form of Annie Fournier appears, along with a couple of handball guards.

"Leave her alone, you hear?" Annie bellows.

Everyone can hear.

"Creep. Leave her alone."

And it's over. Annie and her flanking soldiers march away. The boy picks up his books, and the crowd dissipates. You look at his hair, dark and wild, at the bony shape of his face.

"I am sorry," you repeat, but it is more to yourself than to him. You have broken school protocol in speaking to him at all.

"It's okay. I walk with my eyes closed, too, sometimes."

You want to correct him. You want to tell him you're clumsy, but you look at the rueful acknowledgement on his face and smile.

"Corporeal punishment," he says, and walks past

you. You think about it all day. On the way home on the bus, you pull out your pocket dictionary.

Corporeal—of the human body. Did he use the right word?

You are called into the living room on a quiet Sunday afternoon. There sit your parents, with Annie Fournier between them. It seems that Annie has been taken on to the intramural basketball team, which will mean after-school practice twice a week. As she will miss the bus home and have to be picked up, it only makes sense that you find something to do at the school those afternoons as well.

"Annie says there are all kinds of clubs."

You just bet she has; you can hear the sneering she'd use in the word "clubs."

"So?"

"So join a club."

"I don't want to. I can come home on the bus and do my homework."

But they do not want you home alone after school. Don't they trust you? "Fire Engine Sue", who warned the family and saved the house? That was a million years ago.

"Clubs are good. You get to do things."

Your father this time, looking strange in his new dark turtleneck and bright corduroy trousers.

"I just want to be alone…to read."

Annie offers some helpful advice along the lines of your getting into something basic, then working up to challenges like leatherwork and beading.

"Our busy, busy girls," Robert Cardinal beams, as Annie heads outside to shoot hoops at the newly-mounted basket.

Maybe there's a club for people who want to make crystal radios. Maybe a club for people who trek the mountains barefoot.

You end up nowhere, floating between Sewing for U, where on the cold afternoons you are learning to make a summer blazer, and Skating Techniques, which is theoretical until the ice arrives. After two weeks of shuffling back and forth, you find an empty classroom, sneak in, and close the door.

It is not a room you have ever had a class in. It looks like it could have been a lab once. There's an abandoned hood at the back and a long counter, but then there's also an old movie screen standing crooked on its frame. It is a leftover room, spare chairs end on end, brooms and a mop and a pair of scuffed-up sandals. You sit there until it is time to meet Annie at the showers.

There is more space in the deserted classroom than there will ever be in your bedroom now, so you start bringing your secret book to school on the long days. You also pack the novel, and you are working your way through Mordor one afternoon when you hear faintly and perhaps incorrectly...drums?

Orc drums?

Your school does not have a band. The pathetic music program is run by an old man with asthma who wheezes so loudly that he drowns out Mozart on the *Best of the Classics* album.

You listen.

Sure this time, you open the door of your room and peer down the hall, then tiptoe along the corridor toward the sound. The utility room?

You take a breath and turn the knob.

Cross-legged on the floor, his hair swaying left and right. He looks up.

"You."

"Don't stop…it's nice," you say.

He pauses then resumes his playing. You stand holding the door and listening to him play. When he stops, he hands you his book bag before standing and picking up the bongo drums. He retrieves his bag and is about to depart when you hear yourself say, "Wait. I'll show you where I go."

You lead him back up the corridor.

"Here." You open the door.

"This was always locked. How did you get in?"

"Never locked. Never," you shrug, showing him the lab hood, the broken screen.

"This is great. It would be great to play here."

You are intrigued by the way he never quite looks at you, not head on, but from the side. You realize now the rarity of that first straightforward look, in the cafeteria.

"So you're a drummer, then?"

"Oh…I like guitar, bongos. I like to play…try to play some songs."

"Really? Your own?"

Your own? All he said was "some."

"No…but I like to play T.Rex songs. I play along to

62

them at home."

You imagine, suddenly, a male Annie Fournier, bigger and probably even tougher. Lots of boys. You imagine them jeering at the jittery boy in front of you.

"What's your name?" you ask.

"Dar...Dar Ventner."

"Hi...Dar."

"You?"

"Oh. Suzanne Cardinal."

So we have names.

"What's that band you said?"

He looks right at you again, which startles you, then he lifts up his white school shirt. Underneath it is another shirt with the image of a boyish-looking man, a halo of curls around his head, a starry-eyed expression on his face.

"Marc Bolan. T.Rex. Best band in the universe."

"Best band? What, like The Beatles?"

"They're as big as The Beatles. Uh...not here. In England. In England right now, they're the most popular band."

This is where you fail. At life. At stuff to do with life. Annie Fournier would know this band, and if she didn't, she'd defy his claim and laugh it off. You know so little. Boys. Dancing.

"Sorry, I don't know them."

I don't know anything.

"Nobody much does in Canada or the U.S. The U.S.

is hopeless so far. But in all of Canada, guess where they played?"

You shrug again, picking up an ancient piece of chalk.

"Here…right here. Pierrefonds Arena. September, 1972. I know, 'cause I was there."

"Really?" You move closer to Dar Ventner's voice. "Tell me."

This is the first time you ask him, but it will not be the last. You listen as the young drummer unrolls a spool of colours, guitar-licks, stories about Marc Bolan. You close your eyes and can almost see the crowds, some people with hair like Bolan's, wearing long capes and ruffled shirts. They are timeless, suspended in the Pierrefonds Arena, as an unknown act, The Doobie Brothers, opens the concert.

Dar is there, in the arena, moving about, unable to stand still. Yes, they are standing, all of them. Frustrated with the opening act, which has nothing in common with the music they love, they wait until the first band leaves the stage.

It is noisy and silent, all at once.

"You know what I mean?" Dar asks.

Yes. Like when I get the feeling before I see what's going to happen.

"I think I do…yes."

The stage is bare. Equipment. And then a figure so slight he might be a boy emerges. Thin, delicate. He is more pretty than handsome. The percussionist is handsome.

The delicate boy and the handsome man take the

stage with the other musicians.

"And a one, and a two…"

And the elf springs to life, his guitar sending out electric jerks. He is ripping up and down, like a lightning bolt. The people in the arena catch the current, and soon they are bopping along with him.

He is beautiful. He has glitter on his eyelids. He is a new face that shines.

"Like the Sun King," Suzanne murmurs, remembering her childhood drawing.

Wild. Feral.

"And then, then…" Dar's voice almost a whisper. They are sitting side by side on the floor, their backs up against the supply cabinet.

"…he picks up his acoustic guitar and comes to the edge of the stage. Just him. He sits down, cross-legged, and plays so softly that the audience has to lean forward to hear. One of the new songs, from the *Slider* album, just Bolan and us…."

Bolan and Dar.
Bolan and you.

And he sings "Spaceball Ricochet" as quietly as he cares to, opening a hole in the stratosphere, in his heart, and letting everyone climb in.

Dar moves, startles you. Your eyes open.

"Gotta go. Supposed to be fencing."

"Fencing?"

The Fencing Club, mythic, open only to senior students. Offered by the physics teacher, a former member of Hungary's national fencing team, reportedly a taskmaster both in the classroom and in competition.

"Why'd you skip it, then?"

Dar glances over. "I like it a lot. It's kind of…out there. But today I had to work something out on these," he says, lifting his drums. "Hey, I'm no Bolan or Mickey Finn or anything, but…oh, do you care if I hide them in here? Save me having to carry them home on the bus."

Again the image of a boy, this time with drums, standing at a bus stop, the gang from automotive watching.

"There, under the lab desk. The panel slides shut."

They leave the room together, closing the door softly.

"Well, bye," Dar mutters, turning right down the hall.

You wave and stand watching as he enters the stairwell.

You sit outside the shower room. Annie Fournier appears, all bluster and steam, and hits you on the arm.

"Let's go. Dad'll be out there by now."

In the car, Annie regales Robert Cardinal with the story of her near-perfect basket, with the upcoming game.

"Hey, back there."

Annie Fournier sits in the front now.

"You have any news today?"

You see the bright glint of sword, the impeccable form and exquisite extension.

"Me? No…nothing."

"How's sewing? Anything to show us yet?"

"Nothing yet. Threads."

The sword cuts the Orc in two, rends his face.

Aragorn above him, steady.
Calm.
Dar.

Marc Bolan.
T.Rex.
Spaceball Ricochet.
The Slider.
Dar Ventner.

He tells you things. "Look," he says, "do you see them? They're like us."

And you want to say, "who?" And you want to say, "us?"

They are like him, with clothes inside clothes, secrets, like the lost monks of forgotten tribes. He tells you.

Girls with dark eyes and long heavy skirts, their arms braceletted, black capes and topcoats. Hoods pulled low.

Why?

Boys. Boys free of tug and back-slap, boys with fingernails. Boys with pleats, fine printed shirts, rings and lace and eyelids that shimmer in the stage-light. Boys that are allowed to be pretty. Like Bolan.

You look sideways at Dar.

Dar's fingers are long and thin, the nails on his right hand longer, to pick guitar. He, too, is long and thin, and you can imagine him in bright pants and a silk shirt. His hair is wavy, not like yours, which is like Bolan's, a mess of tiny curls.

"You're lucky," Dar says.

Your hair makes you lucky, you marvel. You envision the people Dar conjures, surely at home in Lothlorien or in any elfin realm.

"They're here," he says. "They're stepping out, like us."

•

You start to look beyond your eyelids now, but the people do not appear. You meet the boy in the empty classroom and listen as he practices a song called "The Planet Queen".

"I don't see them," you tell him. You are making patterns in ancient chalk dust on the blackboard behind the teacher's desk.

"They're here."

Who are they? What are they? What are we? You want to ask.

He never says, but you know he is right. You and he...you are something other than the kids at the bus stop, than Annie and her powerful girlfriends, or the boys who shoulder Dar.

"At the concerts, they're beautiful."

And you want to go to a concert, to see the people of Lothlorien for yourself. But you are young, and you look younger.

Dar tells you of concerts he has read about in England, whole stadiums full of people. And of the small places where people can go and sit in the near dark and watch one another's eyes in the bar light.

He sings the song about the Planet Queen, not to you, but you are there, and when he sings that love is what you want, you close your eyes, and for a moment it is you he means. He sings of dragon heads, machines, and the universe itself reclining in your hair, and you feel yourself expanding, reaching out past the classroom, the school books, the dark thoughts that come flashing. Up into the ionosphere, then into the deep of space.

.

There is a record player in the basement, set up on the stand your father has built over the well pump. It barely qualifies as a stereo, but what do your parents care? Their records range from brittle 78s to the odd foray into "modern" music: Bobby Darin, The Kingston Trio, *Camelot*. This music goes splendidly with the sump-pump's gurgles and the well pump's thumping. Bobby sings about sharks, while in Camelot it never rains. You listen to the description, Camelot the "perfect spot," as you eye the piece of garland stuck since Christmas to the corner of the basement window.

The record player doesn't do the job. It should be able to hold a stack of five LPs at once, above the spinning turntable. It is supposed to drop them one at a time. But Bobby falls on King Arthur, and both are smothered by Mario Lanza.

Despite this, it does play records. Annie Fournier has been acquiring 45s for a while now. She snaps the little plastic plug in the huge hole in the centre and places the tiny record on the turntable. You hear the record playing over and over and over, "You're So Vain", filling the basement as Annie dances around. She is wearing the straw plantation hat from the hatrack and playing plastic castanets as she laughs at your pitiful record collection, two Christmas albums and a Danny Kaye children's story record.

Annie Fournier's 45s are strewn about—Carly Simon, Elton John. Names. As you listen to the song about people who think the song is about them, you block the persuasive voice, close your eyes, and instead see a large place full of people. People like you. They are gazing at the stage, where a young man in a purple satin shirt sits on the floor, his guitar cradled in his lap. He is singing for you, just for you, and you lean against someone's arm and listen.

The boy and the book. Two secrets. You are good at hiding the book, but how will you hide the empty classroom? You have a feeling the boy knows about hiding. He is older than you are. But he is alone, like you.

Meanwhile, victory. Annie Fournier is becoming a star athlete. There is talk of university someday, scholarships, neither of which has ever been mentioned before.

Annie hates school. No, she doesn't hate it. It is just one of the many things she has no respect for, like handcrafted birthday gifts, church and homemade lasagna. But what she does like is the look on Adele and Robert Cardinal's faces when she embroiders her conquests. This is something she has never had. And if it means unfair or specious comparisons to Suzanne, so be it.

In the car, alone with your father, you glance over at the sunglasses that he always wears. His suits have gotten lighter, both in colour and in weight, and he slides into the driver's seat like soft butter onto bread.

"So, what's new in your world?" he says suddenly.

He said "your world."

He can still surprise you. You look sideways at the space between his eyes and his shades.

"The usual...you know."

Does he? He probably doesn't. How could he? You were the oldest, until Annie Fournier. He has no experience.

"Great about...Annie, eh?" he offers.

His eyes blink in the space in front of the glasses.

Thank you. Thank you for not calling her my sister.

You reach over and take a packet of gum from the glove compartment. You peel a Juicy Fruit and angle it into your father's mouth as he tells you about the movie, *The Thin Man,* on TV this week. You still sometimes watch movies together.

Blazer day.
The day the blazer should be done. The sewing instructor doesn't even recognize me any more. Activity module is nearly over.

How will you be able to stay after school now? Your parents don't know the activity session has ended, but Annie does. And if sewing is over, is fencing? For he doesn't always come to see you. He goes to his fencing class as well. And when he does come, he doesn't always talk. Sometimes he just plays. Sometimes he pretends he is playing guitar as his quiet voice sings along to a T.Rex song. You bring an extra snack, an apple or a couple of cookies.

You sit in Algebra working on pairs. You think of pairs as couplets, heroic and otherwise. Maybe you could sign up for something else, as long as they don't check back with the sewing teacher. You wonder what would sound remotely convincing to your parents.

And that is when you realize that you have been lying. It hits hard, because it hasn't felt like lying. You aren't doing anything wrong. But you lie, it seems, to live. To talk to people. To sit with Dar Ventner while he plays music and sings. It has happened so easily. You wake up and write in a secret book, then you go to school and you lie.

Annie Fournier won the Athlete of the Year Award. It's over by her bed. It's shiny. She hangs her sweatband around its neck.

You hurry down the hallway to the deserted classroom. And it is that. Exactly. It is empty.

Blazer day. Fencing day.

When you used to get the feeling, back when you were a kid, it was so overpowering, full of truth. You were bursting with a terrible truth, tongue almost blistering as you expelled it.

But a lie? A lie, you haven't even noticed. Lies are smooth and shapeless. This bothers you, like everything does these days.

The change in your father, into the man about town, as your mother calls him. Or a gadabout, whatever that is. He is not the man who took you bowling, who would find you by the river and walk you home. He is Sir—no—Lord Gadabout. He puts stuff in his hair, on the sides of his head next to his temples. It darkens his hair and confuses you.

"Maybe he's painting his brains," Annie Fournier says.

Your mother is not like that. Your mother changes in ways that are harder to catch. A new dress now and then, but you don't mean that. Your mother tried a hairstyle that was mid-length and nice, but nobody said anything, or maybe they did, and she went back to the pull-off-the-face-and-curl-under helmet.

Of course, Adele Cardinal is not what she once was. Her looks have devolved into a kind of all-purpose acceptability, a non-aggressive attractiveness that suits the mother of teenage girls. She does not turn heads. No one is waiting at work to take her to lunch. Most of the time lunch is a diet shake, anyway, and who wants to share that?

Your mother, if anyone wants to know, watches her husband head for the city and her girls head off to the high school, and she listens, at the table, to the talk show on the radio, staring at her hands and the air that is inside them.

It's like they all breathe different gasses. One inhales oxygen, the other carbon dioxide. People and plants. They're never together on anything. From where you are positioned, you think it looks lonely, and you are becoming an expert on loneliness. You remind yourself that, like plants and people, you are possibly dependent on each other, but this doesn't carry a lot of weight somehow.

You are in the empty classroom after school and you're afraid that it is only a matter of time before you are discovered. You don't spend time here during school hours. Blue-section classrooms are for seniors only, and you only see the seniors in the halls and cafeteria.

You miss him, but that isn't what you mean.

It isn't like Annie and her friends gushing about some basketball player, or Barbara Beauchamp from Grade Ten, suspended for French-kissing Eddy Fredericks in the foyer.

So when he pulls you by the arm over to lockers on your way to English class one afternoon, you don't feel shock or embarrassment. Your body follows your arm.

"Uh…hi. Just thought you'd want to know…got a Bolan import today. My cousin in England sent it. Oh, and this."

Dar Ventner pulls out a small psychedelic patch. A rainbow-coloured Marc Bolan stares out, his eyes hooded beneath the bright embroidery threads.

"Wow."

"You can have it. I got another one. Mine's darker. You can put it on your school bag."

You nod. You have no pack for your books. You still use your father's old attaché case from before his real estate days.

"It's great."

You are about to thank him, but he has already pushed past you and is plowing down the hall. You hold the patch on your open palm as if it is an artifact just uncovered. An arrowhead, or a dinosaur tooth.

Children of the Revolution. Bolan is one of them. Dar. And you?

The raised embroidery might be braille, and you have only to decipher it. You close your hand on the prize then look up to see Annie Fournier watching you.

At home, you sit with the sewing basket.

"Finally," your mother comments. Some work on the invisible blazer.

Safe in your room for the moment, you thread the needle. You cannot match the light gold thread but you can find something neutral.

But sew it on what? There is no way to explain the thing if it is found, nor is there any place on your school uniform or on your home uniform of pants and poor-boy sweater for this patch. You root through your half of the closet. Green shirt? You hate that shirt. The sweater you put on only on coldest days?

The best place for it is the blazer I didn't make. That's where it belongs.
Invisible, like everything.

Where? Jackets can be opened, pullovers pulled over. You choose, at last, a pair of old jeans your mother despises. They're so old, you're not allowed to wear them anywhere but at home, where they are ignored. You sew the face of Marc Bolan inside your jeans and are aware of the strange idea of having his face there, so close to you. You're aware of what people would say if they knew. And when you slip your jeans on and do up the fly, you are aware that this is good, although it is one more secret to add to all the others.

Frog catching.
Jelly making. You would take any course they offered.

"And the sewing class is finished," Annie reports. "All this term's after-school activity classes end at the same time."

Your parents register mild curiosity at this. Annie has filled them in on her competition schedule, outlining the times and her needs. Your needs have been thrown in as a bonus.

"Suzanne, is this true?"

Truth is the thing you have been playing with. It is heavy, and it sinks from sight, whereas the lies bob and float.

"For most kids. I have to stay longer to finish something."

"The blazer?"

"Uh...yeah. They want to put in on display."

"Really? This is great! Is it for parents' night?"

You feel the face of Marc Bolan pressing into you.

"How did you know?"

"This is fantastic!" boasts Robert Cardinal. "Both the girls with something to celebrate. Why don't we go out for dinner?"

The fake Italian place or the Canadian Chinese.

Annie is watching you all the way over in the car. She stares, then glances down at your hands that hold no blazer, then stares, again, at your face.

Broccoli pyramids.
Tortellini towers.
I could build a castle with calabrese rolls.

Dar Ventner is probably in his room with his bongo drums, or tuning up his guitar to practice T.Rex. He is wearing his Marc Bolan badge on a shirt that announces a T.Rex concert in Birmingham. And he's given his extra badge to you.

Mirrors are funny. Look at vampires, they don't show up at all in the glass.

In the song "Jeepster", Bolan says that he is a vampire for her love.

Look at you.

And that he is going to suck her.

•

Punishment.

When had you been planning to tell them? That's what they want to know. Was it in the car, at the door to the school? Or were you planning all along to let them go and make fools of themselves?

"I inquired. I asked the teachers and the vice-principal."

Your mother's face twisted into that of a hurt bird.

"I made them walk me through the entire display in the foyer. And your father…"

"I told them that photos of Annie's team were all well and good, but we wanted to see Suzanne's achievements as well. And do you know what he told me? Do you want to know what the vice-principal said?"

You stare down and feel his hot glare.

"He said, 'and what would those achievements be, Mr. Cardinal?' What achievements!"

"It was just a stupid blazer," you hear yourself mutter.

"Just a…just a…" Mrs. Cardinal rejoins the conversation. "There was no Suzanne Cardinal blazer, because there is no blazer! You realize I had the secretary open her office and search through a stack of lists to find the sewing club registrations? And do you know what the form said?"

You look up. Your mother's face is brilliant pink.

"It said...Suzanne Cardinal—ABSENT, ABSENT, ABSENT. WITHDREW?"

You only notice at this moment that Annie Fournier has crept along the hallway and is at the doorway of the living room. She is conducting the proceedings with a banana, from which she periodically takes a bite.

"We want to know what's going on, Suzanne. You weren't in sewing class. So where were you?"

You look ahead at the rough-edged, impossible truth, at the banana suspended in mid-air.

And lie.

When you were very little, you could hear the birds talking. They spoke to each other and to the frogs by the river. Sometimes the river talked as well. And if·you were extremely quiet, you were able to hear the wavy grass whisper along the banks.

Carla talked to everything. She chattered to the crayons in your green pencil box. She talked to her dolls. She burbled like the swirly part of the river.

And now, now when you stare at the pinched face of your mother, you can't remember the first thing about it.

I opened my mouth, but nobody heard me. I talked, but Charlie Donaldson fell.

They have no words for you any more. Your father has thrown up his hands in despair—or is it anger?— for you cannot read the expression that has congealed on his face. Your mother, as well, is speechless. I want, I want, I want...what do you want? A blazer to wipe away the tears?

Face it. Face it.

The only one who looks at you now is Annie Fournier. She stares at this replica of deceit, and smiles. She moves her stuff off the floor in front of your bed. There is something devious in the thought of this girl lying to her own parents, something that captures the respect of the five-foot-eleven-inch basketball star.

"Right to their faces! And that hokey story about spacemen or whatever it is you said. Cosmic do-da, creatures drumming, music coming out of the walls. Hah! You're a liar or you're crazy. You know, boom-boom, ain't it great to be crazy?"

Annie punches the air. Boom-boom.

Mrs. Reidel always told you to listen carefully. Get in close. You listen now, but all you hear is *Three's Company* on TV. Annie has gone to practice. Your parents are two stone-headed people. You try and try but you cannot hear the stones.

It is cold by the river, the wind whipping the clouds into a froth. Birds are keeping to themselves and frogs are neither seen nor heard. You walk along the bank, bend, and cup your hands in the frigid water.

The river was sad today.
Nobody talks to me.

What's it say in that song?
"I'm alone and I'm unseen."
What would Marc Bolan say?
Or D.V.

You try not to think about the boy, as he is part of your untruthful life. You thought about him as you were lying, as your parents' eyes narrowed. But he exists only if you lie.

Like everything.

Annie Fournier comes bombing down the hall between classes and spots you muddling your way through with a book to your face.

"Good way to get killed," she says, almost cheerfully. "Are you ever going to finish that thing?"

You have long ago left the Shire but are still making your way to Mordor.

"I don't have practice after school. It's been cancelled," Annie announces.

"So?"

"We're not going to tell anyone that, are we?"

"What?"

Your nose comes up to Annie Fournier's collar-bone.

"We're not going to tell them. Why waste perfectly good freedom, right? You can say you stayed late to watch the practice. I'll meet you back here at five thirty. A little time off for good behaviour. What do you think?"

"But...what do we do?"

"*We* don't do anything. I'm meeting some friends at the Chicken. You can do whatever you like. Talk to aliens. Whatever. Look, I'm giving you an excuse, here."

You nod. You re-stack your books and pencil-case. You watch Annie Fournier move off down the corridor, one or two students peeling off to the sides in her wake. She's a speedboat on a small river, loud, dangerous and wrong.

All the same, you cannot concentrate for the entire afternoon. Your geography quiz is sitting on your desk half-done, your head definitely in the frothing clouds along the river. Or in the airless, empty classroom in the senior's hall.

You want to be the Planet Queen that Bolan sings about, to wear shiny silver garments that move the way you do. To have a flying saucer come and take you away. Everything would be fine. But you are not beautiful, not a "Cool Motivator", like Bolan wants. You are Suzanne, and you are on your way to detention for lack of attention in class.

Detention. There's Mary Foley from French class. The French teacher hates Mary's pathetic accent. And Cheryl and Gail, who are always in trouble. But the other faces are strangers, other hopeless and brainless ones like you, removed from the herd. Your one chance to check the classroom, and you are in study hall.

Someone has written the national anthem on the board. What is this classroom used for? You sing "O Canada" in your head, in English and in French, pausing as you always do at the image of the French people carrying the cross, or is it swords and a cross? The words are different in English. Imagine. The anthem means different things in each language.

You finish your math homework, so the period is not a total loss. It is nearly half-over when he walks in. Dar

Ventner passes a slip of paper to the teacher and starts down the first aisle. He's wearing his T.Rex shirt beneath the getting-too-small white shirt, and the pants are as strange as ever, the ones with the invisible seams and fasteners. The pack on his back has writing on it, handwritten slogans, as well as a T.Rex emblem. He is partway down the aisle when he spots you on his right. Something like recognition hits his face. Is it a smile?

Dar Ventner cuts diagonally through the desks, tripping over a briefcase, and claims the desk next to yours. Study hall rules include silence, so he merely gestures to you with two fingers, a peace sign, before setting up his books.

Whenever you arrived at Mrs. Reidel's house, everything seemed immediately better. Ferg would meow and fuss, of course, but you were welcome there.

Now, with Dar Ventner beside you in a quiet study hall, something other than comfort, but comforting nonetheless, comes calling. You can see his left hand writing in his exercise book, the long fingers that should be playing guitar or drums. He has a bruise on the wrist, as if someone has wrenched it. An Indian sunburn gone wrong?

You work side by side as the period ticks by.

"Class…well, you're hardly a class, are you? A collection of miscreants culled from the ranks. You are dismissed, and I hope never to have the pleasure of your company again."

The regulars snigger, and the mumbling picks up as bags are packed.

Dar Ventner opens his sack to deposit his books, and a newspaper clipping appears in his hand. He places the paper on your desk. The photo is of Marc Bolan and Mickey Finn, T.Rex, at a recent venue in Britain.

You trace your finger along the wavy black outline of Bolan's hair.

"Cool," you mutter.

"I'm saving it," he takes it back.

You nod. "Do you...do you ever go to the classroom?"

Dar Ventner looks at you through the long veil of hair in front of his eyes. "Seem to be here these days."

He shrugs, and while it isn't a smile, exactly, he bares his teeth a fraction.

"I...uh," you can't believe you're telling him this. "I sewed the Bolan patch...inside my jeans."

He leans in and is about to say something, then changes his mind. His hand with the bruise brushes your arm. "See you."

You wait for Annie Fournier, who is late getting back from the chicken place. Annie babbles on about you both having to get your stories straight and even offers you the rest of her Coke. You nod and shake your head on cue and are wordless all the way home in the car.

"I said, how does she look in practice?"

Annie turns and shoots you a glare.

"Oh...uh...amazing. She's a star, you know that."

Now both father and Annie are smiling.

See you.
And he does. He is the only one who does.

It has not happened in so long. It *can't* be back. You send your covers flying; sweat is in your eyes.

Get up!

You sit upright in the dark room. The window is a filmy shade of grey. Pre-dawn.

Salt? No, a bitter, bitter taste in your mouth.

I've been eating cars. I've been eating the bumpers of cars.

There is a difference between dreams and the other thing. Dreams are Annie Fournier and team winning the Canadian championships, or Robert Cardinal returning with a boat and motoring down the river in his blue socks and brown sandals. Dreams are Dar Ventner and a music festival.

You shiver uncontrollably. The metal taste is leaving, but the image of the cars remains. You wipe your face on your top sheet and crawl out of bed. The house is silent. Annie Fournier sleeps through anything. Your parents are asleep. It is at moments like these that you are grateful you have no pet.

The kitchen is gun-metal dull. It is precisely fourteen steps to the fridge, where you find then pour yourself a glass of grapefruit juice. The sour liquid hits your tongue, and you are thankful. It hits your stomach, which turns upon itself and drops you down to a crouch. You squeeze your eyes and look out the window. Early birds are already flitting and flapping at the bird-feeder. Sparrows are so needy. You thought there was a brown rabbit a moment ago, but it is only a mound of dirt left by your father's aggressive lawn mower, which shaves the tops off small rises in the terrain. The birds eat and eat as the birdbath on the lawn beckons.

What was it?

You are afraid to go into that place of light. Your

head aches, all of your senses, in fact, are ragged. Eyes, ears. The tips of your fingers are on fire.

Sit.

Sit with your eight-ounce glass of grapefruit juice. Breakfast is the most important meal of the day.

You feel someone jostle you, look up and see your mother, hair still in curlers.

"You're up early," Adele says, heading to the kettle.

You straighten. You must have dozed, right there at the table, like Mrs. Reidel in her chair.

Your mother removes two slices of bread from the plastic bag and pops them into the toaster. Soon you smell coffee and toast, and if you stay any longer you will smell peanut butter.

"What? Not even going to have breakfast? You should eat, Suzanne."

"Yeah, Suzanne," Annie Fournier muscles past her in her baby-doll pyjamas.

Out behind the house, the sky is darker. No bird feeders here, and so no birds. The bushes are stunted this year from lack of rain. Or the fact that nobody ever looks at them, not even the animals.

No. Maybe plants don't need anybody. They live their whole lives just...living. Not crying. Not lying. Not shivering.

I have been eating cars.

In English class you are reading "Leiningen Versus the Ants", a story about a man who builds great fortifications to protect himself from an invasion of killer ants. The insects destroy everything: the plantation, the crops, in the end—almost the man. You are not sure but think it is supposed to be a story about how mankind survives anything. Something like that. English class is full of stories about people who live through a shipwreck, battle, injustice. Math class is about facts.

Face them.

Your father has come home this evening in a buoyant mood. He has been offered a promotion at the real estate company. How do you get promoted? Do you get to sell bigger houses? Use bigger signs? The new job will mean more money. It will also involve a move to the city.

"I want to sit down like a family and discuss this," he says, but his eyes are watching a movie playing on his lenses.

You shift to look at your mother. The face, as always, is unreadable; not blank, but revealing nothing.

"Well? I'm listening," your father says.

"Cool," Annie Fournier replies.

Annie Fournier. You know it is different for her. How many times has Annie moved?

"Adele? You're pretty quiet."

Now an expression that passes for mystery moves across her mother's face. Can she have no opinion on this news?

"It's a big step, Robert."

"Sure it is! Sure it is! It's just the kind of step we should be taking. The girls are older...there's more to do in the city. Think of the advantages! You could even find something part-time if you wanted. Eh?"

He is playing that card. You watch.

"I...I don't know. When do you have to let them know?"

You hear them talking. There are so many things to consider. Your mother has wanted to go back to work. The kids. The house.

You leave them to it and return to the essay you are writing for English.

Leiningen's barrier of fire fails to stop the ants because...

We are moving. I get my own room in the new house.
I get to go to school on my own, on a city bus. Or I can walk there if I want.

You have not been down by the cemetery in a long time. It isn't that you're afraid; you're not one of those people who think these places are haunted. Or, rather, that only these places are. This is the cold, windy kind of day things would happen, though. The funny thing is, when you first came here, you didn't know any of the names. There was just a deep hole. Your white gloves got dirty, and your mother slid them off and beat them against a tombstone.

Now as you move between the rows, you know names. Mrs. Craig from the library. Mr. Smith, the bus driver.

You stop in front of Mrs. Reidel's stone.

"We're moving," you whisper.

You wish that Ferg the cat were still here.

"We're going to the city."

It takes you longer than you thought to get to Carla. The section is a little overgrown. They used to come and clip around the stone. Nobody does that any more?

Carla's stone is not fancy. You remember your mother, at the time, saying fancy would be inappropriate for a child, then breaking down and having to be helped to the sofa. Carla's stone is small and white. Her name is in plain letters, but there is a bird carved on the stone. It hits you, all of a sudden, that the bird is a cardinal. In all the years, you have never realized that. You kneel before the grave, holding your hair back from your eyes in the wind.

"We're starting over," you say.

You have never skipped a regular class before. It is one thing after school, but this? The halls are patrolled by monitors, and the penalty for unauthorized presence in the corridor, without a note, is an immediate, escorted trip to the principal's office.

You don't care. You will be leaving this school soon. You make your way down the hallway that you only used to visit after hours. It is not empty now—there are classes going on in almost every room. The door to the classroom at the end of the hall is shut.

As you creep along, you wonder whether it would do any good at all to tell them you don't want to go. But you know. Your mother has applied for work in the city; your father has bought two new suits. The sign on the front lawn makes it pretty official as well.

"FOR SALE BY OWNER."

"I'm *in* real estate! I can sell my own stupid house!"

The stupid house is up for sale.

You try the door to the classroom. It opens with a soft click. One quick glance behind you, then you are inside. The dull light from the small upper windows diffuses through the dark space. You sit at a front desk staring at the empty board.

Except it isn't empty. A small circle has been drawn in the corner. In it a crudely-drawn outline. You know the shape. It is the outline of Marc Bolan's head on the T.Rex crest you wear in your jeans. Yes, the curve of Bolan's halo of hair. Beneath the circle, this: *2:30 today.*

When was this written? You check your watch. It is 2:15—today? You shiver and wrap your arms around yourself.

When he arrives, you try not to act surprised.

"Glad you could make it," he says, sitting on the teacher's desk in front of you. "When I...wrote that...I didn't know if you were still coming here or not."

"No," you sputter. "I mean, me neither."

He seems agitated. You can see something ugly on his forehead when he shakes his head.

"What...where did you get that?"

You forget that you are Suzanne and approach him, touch his forehead. He flinches.

"Where did you get it?"

He manages a half-smile. "Oh...a few of the fans."

He turns away, closing in on himself.

"You should...somebody should look at that. Did you see a doctor?"

Somebody should look at it.

"It's okay," he says. He's looking up at the tiny squares of light.

You wonder what his family thinks of this. How can they not notice? You think of Dar, how he is, how he would probably tell them it's an injury from fencing. You know how he would do it. You do it too. You want to sit with him, to hear him play, to listen to music and drift away from this dusty, dirty place.

"I'm moving," you say. No matter how many times you hear yourself, you can't believe it's true.

He looks over, eyes wide. "When?"

"City. My dad has this job."

Did you think he would be upset? Angry? Did you think he would care?

"I'll never get out of here," he says.

"What?"

"Me. I'll never get out of this friggin' place."

His face is obscured by the hair. He is no longer even attempting to imitate the school dress code, his pants lime green with stripes, his shirt a head-shot of Marc Bolan and Mickey Finn, T.Rex, on tour somewhere in England. She can see the glint of an earring in his right ear.

"You're the only one," you almost whisper.

"What?"

You are staring at him, not believing your brashness.

"The only one who's ever talked to me in this whole…friggin' place."

You can see one half of a smile.

"Are you going to be okay?" you say before you can stop yourself. What are you, his mother? You can't forget the bruises he hides so poorly.

He only shrugs and performs a little percussion on the desktop. "Lunacy's Back," he sings. It is a Bolan song from an early album, you know. You know more than you thought you did.

You take the record he offers you, take his hand. You take all the pain in his face. But you have nothing to give. So you tell him about Fire Engine Sue. The years of silence tumble out into his hands, and he holds them with you. He looks at you strangely, it is true, but he does not pull away.

"You tell the future."

"Some, only a few, times."

He nods as if he understands how there are some people with futures that are visible, some with futures that are shadows in laneways. You don't say any more about it, but you feel the bag of heavy fish lifting off your chest, the silver flicking bodies you have had to fight so long.

He held onto my hand. We didn't hold hands.
He held on hard like we were about to leap off the
edge of the world and into the sky.

"She's got a boyfriend. That's why she doesn't want to leave."

Annie Fournier is practicing a sideways karate kick on the frame of the kitchen doorway.

"What?" Adele Cardinal's head turns like Linda Blair's in *The Exorcist.*

"Really?"

The smile is part hungry, part horrific, as if its owner is perplexed.

"Get lost!" you sputter. "You're full of it!"

"I'm only saying what I've heard. Julie McCarthy said she saw you with some creep in the hall."

"Julie McCarthy's full of it."

"Or maybe you're full of it. Full of luuuuuvvvv..."

"Stop it!" Adele shouts. "Stop...Sue...Suzanne. Is it true?"

She might as well be asking if you have cancer, with that look on her face.

"No," staring at your mother straight on. "No, I don't have a boyfriend. As if anyone would go out with me."

"As if," Annie lunges, her foot just missing your head.

We move tomorrow. The desk is moving, too, so I'll be able to keep my diary. But I'll have to take it with me in my pack. The principal was sad to see Annie Fournier go. The principal said, and I quote: "Star athlete, school spirit, lots of enthusiasm." And about me: "Math marks up, quiet but unmotivated—counselling?"

That night there is another dream; this time it is not cars. You are standing by a road. It's night, yet all the birds are singing mournfully. It sounds like untamed flutes and piccolos. There are flashing lights that are beautiful, but somebody is crying. You look around in the thick muslin night. The crying is rich and full.

You wake up and vomit on the floor where the bedside rug had been only the day before. Bare room now, cold wooden floor, and Annie Fournier snoring in her corner.

In the bathroom, you wash out your mouth and get a wet towel to wipe up the floor. The house is a voodoo town, a warehouse of boxes. There are no curtains on the windows, and the wind whips branches in front of your face. You stand in the dark holding the towel, looking at the silhouette of boxes and the wild dancing branches behind them.

•

The new room. It's ivory, but I can paint it if I want. Blue, maybe, or orange. Not allowed orange. Paint It Black, like

*Annie says. Annie Fournier wanted this room, but I was
standing in it, blocking the door. She was looking over my
shoulder at the window, and the closet, and I thought they
were going to make me give it to her, but they didn't.*

The new room is emptier without Annie Fournier.
Annie's room is green, a puke green that you hated on
sight. Annie's tape deck is already set up, and music
blares down the hall. Soon she will put up her
posters—basketball stars, pop groups, something
stupid like an Iron Butterfly album cover, just to look
cool. Soon her KEEP OUT sign will reappear, probably
on the door to her bedroom this time, instead of
idiotically above her bed in the old room.

Adele Cardinal is flying through the house like a
demented bat, bolts of cloth unfurling in her
slipstream. Do bats have slipstreams? She seems to
want to reinvent this house, to erase all evidence of the
former owners and paint, upholster, fringe and chintz
her way into a born-again house. You are reminded of
the bag of cut-up material that would have been your
blazer. Maybe there could even be a use found for that,
a little soft-sculpture of failure.

The house is on a residential street that feeds into a
busy thoroughfare. When you listen for it, you can hear
the traffic, only a block or so away. You cannot hear birds
or dogs. You are sure there are no frogs to listen for.

You and Annie will begin school the coming week. It
is ironic that although you are in the city now, your
school is actually smaller than the last one. A local high
school, not a regional one. A walk to school, not a bus
ride. A pair of jeans, not a uniform.

You think of Dar Ventner, his green pants, the broken dress code and the bruised wrist and forehead. Is he still in school, or has he been kicked out?

I can wear my jeans in school, the ones with Bolan inside.

Wandering, strolling through a new neighbourhood alone. There is a convenience store at the end of the street, just around the corner. It has coffee and ice cream and cigarettes and things people can't do without. You have already seen Annie Fournier buying a pack of cigarettes there. She looks older than she is, whereas you…

Athletes shouldn't smoke.
Well, nobody should smoke, but athletes need to breathe.
What an idiot.

Before long, your mother lands a job in the competitive world of direct sales. This is what she calls it —the competitive world of direct sales. A resort north of the city is offering package discounts for ski vacations in winter and spa vacations in summer. All Adele Cardinal has to do is convince people that they have the time and the money to grab this deal while it's hot.

Your father has congratulated her on this new position, although he admits to a strong preference for real estate.

"Real estate. It's real. I show them actual houses."

Adele shrugs, look at her, less impressed than he would like. "So? I deal in dreams. The dream of finding the perfect man in the lounge *après* ski. The dream of rekindling a flagging romance in the hot tub, with complimentary champagne."

"Well, I guess you have to believe that to sell it. Sounds like you rehearsed it."

"Not at all!" Adele stands. She looks taller since accepting the job. Her hair is better, too. Strange, as it is telephone sales. "I really believe this, Robert. That's what will make me effective in sales."

"You really believe in…?"

"In the perfect vacation, yes. Yes, I do."

You look back from your mother's face to your father's. How will he respond?

Your father smiles wryly. "I thought you meant the perfect romance."

Adele Cardinal checks the waist and zipper of her skirt and heads to the front closet. She can get the bus from the corner, and in only twenty minutes is at work at Marvel Tours. Robert Cardinal will take the car, as he has to show a house. How convenient it is that the girls can walk to school.

You leave before Annie does. It isn't calculated, it just is. You like seeing the stores before they open shop. So much promise in the windows. The tiny park with the two benches is deserted. In your mind, you always claim one of the benches as your own, although during the day it is occupied by an elderly man who has nothing better to do than sit. It is empty now, and you amble up to it. You drape your arms over the back of the bench as you have seen one of the old men do.

You own this park.

At eight fifteen in the morning, you own this park. The Planet Queen's realm.

•

When you rise from the bench, two years have passed. Insane—how can two years have slid by so surreptitiously? Everything has changed. Everything and nothing. Your father is having an affair; you are sure of this. Annie Fournier plays ball for the city as well as the school, and she is being courted provincially, and your bedroom has been converted into an exercise room for her.

You sleep in the basement now, in the partially-finished and partially-furnished panelled corner. Which is okay. You can spread out down there and play your music, which was hard to do upstairs, as it competed with Annie's.

Because nothing has changed but everything has. You wear magical clothes now, at home and at school. Your mother hates them but hates the arguments more. Your long hair is thick with tight, frizzy curls; your nails are green or blue or whatever colour you "feel" that day. You listen to Bolan, to T.Rex, to David Bowie, to Roxy Music. Annie has written you off as a glam queen imposter, a loser.

But you have discovered the truth about silence. It is beautiful. They burble and squawk around you, demanding and accusing. But inside, in the monastery, inside walls, there is a courtyard with an orange tree.

1975. Book three. Funny.
Love takes a holiday.
I'm on crazy duty
Dah-dah-dah-Hah!

Your grades have bottomed out at school, where you
are regarded as intelligent but vacuous, energetic but
unfocussed. A waste. They don't agree about you at all.
You float through the classrooms in Indian cotton
shirts, in clinking beads and bracelets. What is that
cloyingly sweet scent you wear?

At home, everyone tries to ignore you. It isn't hard,
since you basically live in the basement. You come up
for meals, not speaking, and disappear again. One
strange thing, though; you always wash the dishes after
supper. You finish, turn, half-bow to your mother, as if
to an elder or a mentor, and clear out.

Adele is beyond wondering. She is too busy for this,
too harried at work, where she manages in-city
advertising for a resort in the mountains. She wishes
Robert would pick up the slack, but he's never available.
Sometimes Adele wishes he'd never taken the city job, but
there is no denying their lifestyle is up since the move. At
least they don't have to worry about Annie. She's on track
and is likely to receive an athletic scholarship when she
graduates. It's difficult, but they do attend her games
when they can. Adele does, anyway. Robert, too, on
occasion. Suzanne's hopeless. Just as well. In that
ridiculous get-up, she would only embarrass them.

You smile. Silence.

Robert feels the same. That is, when he communicates
with his family at all. It is hectic, leading a double life. All
it means, some days, is two sets of lies. But he and his
mistress have been together for some time, and she
doesn't complain as much as she could. Besides. Besides.
He wonders what it would be like if he were found out, if
the two separate vehicles collided. He doesn't necessarily

want to lose anybody, not Adele or...Angela. When he allows himself, he thinks: I'm still in the A's.

You know this, and you watch your father, silent.

The days slide by. You go from intense moments listening to music and writing, to numb hours in school. Whoever invented school couldn't have meant this. Your head is exploding, but all that is visible is the kid with the hair and the goofy clothes, the kid who never talks. You are reading a book about meditation. You are flipping through books, *The Electric Kool-Aid Acid Test* and *Thus Spake Zarathustra.* People ignore you.

Once a boy stood by your desk before the bell rang. He was flushed, and fringed with pimples. He stammered, "Wanna go to the dance on Friday?"

You stared at your Bic pen, frozen. Your ears buzzed. You could not say a word. The boy stood awkwardly a moment longer, then shuffled away.

What was that? Did it really happen?

Your journal page blank for the rest of that day.

Annie Fournier is seeing a hockey jock. It is all so easy; you could predict it in your sleep. Annie and the muscled defenseman. What do they possibly talk about? Do they talk at all, or is it just pawing and sweating?

Stop it.

You try to be fair. Annie is...your eyes open wide as you realize you were almost going to walk past the invisible barrier.

•

How they find you is anybody's guess. Eventually you piece together something about the school and the principal, but at the time you have no idea how you are able to open the door one afternoon before supper and discover the small woman in the knit hat standing there. There is hope and pain in the woman's eyes. You recognize it immediately. The woman tells you she is Dar Ventner's mother.

You sit in the living room. You are no good at this; should you offer tea or a handshake, or even manners?

Dar Ventner is in the hospital in the city. His mother thinks he is going to die.

"What?"

You reach instinctively for the patch you wear close to your heart. It is the Marc Bolan patch Dar gave you, and it has been sewn and re-sewn on clothes as you have grown.

Dar Ventner is in hospital, and he is going to die.

"He said he knew you lived here somewhere. He asked me to find you. It's taken time; I've spent so much time…"

"I'm sorry," you say, and reach out to hold the woman's hand in yours. Your green fingernails enfold the woman's small clenched fist.

In the taxi to the hospital, the woman tries to make conversation. Who are you, and why has her son never mentioned you before? She knows you went to school together, but you seem a little young to have been in any of her son's classes.

Who are you?

The small owl-face with the red-rimmed eyes imploring.

You have no time to prepare.

You have not seen Dar Ventner in two years. You enter the room, remembering the citrus-ammonia-caramel-diaper smell, the way Mrs. Reidel smelled when she came home from the hospital.

"Darren," the owl woman says. "I've brought the girl."

You approach.

As you step closer, you see in a flash your last strange dream at the old house, the dirge-singing birds, the woman crying. Why hadn't you known? The dark night, the mourning, the woman is a girl, is you. The broken starfish on the ground is Dar Ventner, hair streaming out behind his unrecognizable face, his long hands, his lovely fingers cracked.

Dar's mother is in the corner, looking out the window. There is now.

"Dar...Dar..."

You are afraid to touch this pain, yet you place your hand like a snowflake on his arm. A gurgle catches somewhere in his throat. "...found you..."

You are outraged. You want to rip the tubes out, punch something, anything. "Who did this?"

But you know, your tears spilling onto his bandaged right arm, the left one in traction.

Another gurgle. It almost sounds like a sneeze or even a laugh. "F...fans..."

He says nothing more for a long time. Mrs. Ventner goes out to make a call. The nurse comes in to check on Dar and looks at you disapprovingly.

"Family?" she demands.

You have not taken your eyes off Dar. You hover by him, by the bandages of the skinny boy who plays guitar and drums. The hospital gown is foolish on him, its stupid diamond print with dots. His hair is damp and back off his face, the way he would never wear it. Forehead bandaged. His nose is broken, you think, though you have never seen a broken nose.

When you sat beside him on the classroom floor, he let your body bump up against his, like you were two boats moored side by side. A wave, a thought, would pass between you and your bodies would brush up, bits of wood splintering, paint peeling, as you shared space.

You shared space.

His hand, gently, now.

You are remembering the Bolan song about God. About the boy who is like a boat. He is like a boat because he, too, is sunk.

Mrs. Ventner sits in the gold vinyl chair, styrofoam coffee listing dangerously.

"He never...you never came over. He never mentioned you."

She is struggling to comprehend you, your funny hair and clothing, your thin young presence. You reach forward to right the coffee cup, take it from Mrs. Ventner and place it on the end table.

"I knew Dar from school...the regional."

"I know that!" the woman snaps. Then, "I'm sorry, dear. I don't know what I'm doing."

Your hands go back to the woman's, and she holds you like she held the cup.

A hiccup sound and a rapid sucking in of air.

"No. They have no leads. They say it could be anybody. How could it be anybody?"

She has lost her hold, this woman, and is falling into the abyss. You stand up and reach an arm around the woman's shoulders.

"If only he didn't provoke...wearing those stupid rags and wandering around...if only he wasn't so odd all the time, like he..."

And it is as if she is seeing you for the first time.

"But you're like him as well, aren't you?"

You see both of you, eyes closed, on the floor of the deserted classroom. He is talking about lost lands and mythical maidens.

"Yes, Mrs. Ventner. I'm like him."

You are in the hallway, at the end of the hallway, poking a finger through the metal grating on the window. Who is it protecting? The healthy people outside? You listen to the noise, the air conditioner or converter, or whatever the dragon's roar is. Are they trying to keep the people in here from flinging themselves out over the avenue?

You are in the middle of your attempt at removing the grating when you hear the shriek. Mrs. Ventner.

Dar.

You rush back to the room but cannot penetrate the sudden pall. Mrs. Ventner in suspended animation above her son's body. You want to tell her to stay there, don't look down. Wile E. Coyote is always safe in mid-air until he looks down. But she must look down.

And they've killed her too.

You've seen that face before, your mother on the

edge of Carla's grave. So easy to fall in, the ground giving way, clumps of earth hitting the wedge of a white box. You hear the clumps, their thud on something that is almost hollow.

You stay with Mrs. Ventner until Dar's father arrives. You don't know why, but you read a lot into this Mr. Ventner, a tall, well-dressed man with glasses and slightly hunched shoulders. His face is expressionless, or expressionless considering. He has in tow a young boy, aged maybe six. The boy has Dar's long fingers, his questioning eyes. He is introduced as Casey, and he is not crying, but he has registered the dismay in the hallway and is afraid to go into the room.

"I can stay with him, if you like," you offer.

The parents mutely depart.

"Hi...uh, you want to go sit over there?"

The boy follows you and sits beside you on the vinyl chairs.

"I'm...I'm a friend of Dar's," you say.

"Me too," the boy nods. "Darren is my big brother."

"I know."

He's so little.

"He got hurt, you know."

"Yeah, I know."

The slender fingers knot around the arm of the chair. "Dad says he was stupid."

"What?"

"Dad. He says he knew something like this would happen."

An oracle? A freak like her? Or just someone with Big Fear and...

"No. Casey? No. Your brother was not stupid. Dar's

not…he's a good guy, you know?"

The boy examines the seams of the chair. "Yeah. He always sings to me."

"Really?" You draw nearer. "Tell me about that, Casey."

"He…sings these songs. Sometimes he plays guitar or his bongos."

"Know something?" You are hugging him now. "He used to do that for me, too. Isn't that neat?"

You sit together until Mrs. Ventner returns.

"Darren's father is going to stay with him awhile," she whispers, then turns to her other son. "So, have you been a good boy?"

Casey allows his mother to lift him up into her arms. "Yes, Mommy. Just like Darren."

Mrs. Ventner's tears spill onto the young boy's head.

Of course, you have no explanation as to why you weren't at home to receive the time-sensitive papers your father was having delivered. You haven't worked on your term paper and will be up all night.

"Are you going to tell us what's going on?" your father demands.

You could say the same to him, have him tell everyone about his pathetic affair with the pasty woman downtown. They are so useless. They have been seen by everyone, it seems, except the blind and definitely dumb Adele.

"Suzanne?"

What's it to be? Another lie to add to the pile of them out back? "I was at the hospital."

"What?" Your mother leaps up from her chair.

"I was visiting a friend."

"Who?"

"You don't know him."

"*Him!*" your mother says.

You look at them, so sure of everything. "He was my friend, and he died."

Annie surely thinks you're joking, because she says, "Fire Engine Sue's friends all die."

Your mother is horrified.

The story comes out, the boy at the old school, a friendship, just a friendship, after all, and his death.

"I don't understand," your mother says.

Your father rises and goes to the living room, returning with a drink, which he downs in one gulp.

You want to go to the funeral.

"Where? Back in town? Why? You said you hardly knew him. Why put yourself through that?" Robert asks. He should just bring the bottle in rather than making all those trips.

"He made you cut classes," Adele is saying. "Is he the one who got you interested in this awful dress-up you do?"

"It's disrespectful to go to the funeral if you're not close to the deceased."

"Probably taught you to smoke as well. Did he get you to smoke?"

"You can send a card of condolence to the family."

"How did they find your address to reach you? Were you seeing him secretly?"

You close your eyes. A new voice. Annie's. "She should go."

Everyone looks at her.

"She should go. It's important to say goodbye."

105

The following weekend, your father drives you to
the funeral. It is difficult for both of you to be there. He
doesn't like having to think of the wasted years when
he sat at home in a daze. He doesn't want to think of
how dependent he was back then. Adele. He waited for
her every day. He waited for Little Sue. Whereas the girl
by his side is anybody's guess.

At your mother's insistence, you have toned down
your outlandish clothes. You are in simple mourning
clothes, as your mother assures you many others will
be, and you have removed the multi-coloured nail-
polish. Black slacks, your mother's black sweater, your
hair tied back. It will have to do.

"You want me to go with you?" He doesn't want to
go, he doesn't even want to be here.

"No...Dad, I'm okay."

He is surprised and looks grateful. "Okay. Good," he
says softly, and for a second you are as you used to be,
sharers of secrets, allied against enemies.

"I'll drive around and go for a drink. I'll meet you
back at four."

You are on your own. It is the height of irony that
although Dar Ventner did not live in your old town, he
came here after he died. The regional school "collected
punks", as her Latin teacher called them, from all over.
But Dar's father had come from this area, and this is
where Dar would be buried.

As Dar's coffin enters the church, you are shocked to
see a silver unicorn painted on the side, like those long
stretchy lions she's seen on the standards of kings. She
doesn't know the pallbearers, except for Mr. Ventner,

who stoops even more with this weight on his shoulders. They place the coffin on the bier, and it slides forward. Little Casey sits with his mother, who looks back as the casket makes its way up the aisle. She sees you and nods in your direction.

The unicorn is mesmerizing. Who gave permission for that? You never knew people were allowed to paint on coffins. You would have made some flowers on Carla's for sure. Or a frog. You look from Mrs. Ventner to the stolid face of Dar's father.

They hate the unicorn. They did it for Dar.

You see your former school principal, who gives you a stiff acknowledgement.

The service begins.

Oh, Dar.

You arrange your scratchy sweater and can feel the Marc Bolan patch on your left breast. You try not to see the purple flesh, the meaty fingers. There is a police investigation.

Tell them to look for the fans.

You know.

The organ is playing, something that the program says is from Bach. It is okay. But in your head, it is Marc Bolan singing "Cosmic Dancer".

Your father has not wanted to have to meet you at the cemetery, so you've arranged to be picked up at the convenience store.

Afraid. He's chicken.

You have time enough to wander from the mound of dirt beside Dar's place over to Carla's. It has been a while. The weeds around Carla's stone are stubborn.

You bend down to grab them and pull. Carla pulls back.

It's me. Little Sue.

You work until the stone is free of grass and timothy.

"Excuse me."

You turn.

"Sorry..." Mrs. Ventner is standing there, holding a large bag. "I was afraid you'd left."

Only now does she glance at the stone, reading it and look at you with wider, wetter eyes. She thrusts the bag forward. "These are for you. I think he'd want you to have them."

You stand and wipe grass from your hands. The blades fall at an angle.

You reach for the bag. "What...?"

The bag contains records, T-shirts, clippings.

"Oh."

So when Robert Cardinal manages to meet you later at the convenience store, you haul the bag into the car and smell the air to determine how much he has had to drink.

"Was it okay?" he asks, navigating a lane change.

This is when you wish you were old enough to drive. "Yeah. They played Bach."

"Oh. Good. What did you buy?"

You shift the bag. "This. Nothing. Souvenirs," you say, and close your eyes.

He had a good collection, and you play the records constantly. Even from the basement, it is starting to annoy everybody. You have memorized "Children of the Revolution" and sing it to yourself as you move around the subterranean bedroom.

Annie says that Bolan sounds like a Munchkin.

"Does not!" you yell.

You want to be one of the children of the revolution, and you are dying in this house.

"He's a fairy."

Annie Fournier has dumped the hockey player and is in the market for another boyfriend. She appraises every male. And she hates the artsy types, the skinny, pale boys with curly hair and hooded eyes. She likes boys who sweat, swear and shower, who grunt when the puck or the ball is passed to them. She has seen photos of Marc Bolan, delicate-faced.

"Fairy."

"You shouldn't," you whisper. "You shouldn't call people names."

"Sticks and stones," Annie sneers.

Sticks and stones and words and fists.

Your journal is empty for the day Dar died. His funeral date is also blank.

"Really, Suzanne, your marks have to pick up. You don't want to be taking classes in the summer, do you?"

They are talking to you.

"Put down the book and look at me, Suzanne."

They are pointing at her report card. Look at those grades.

"What are you going to do about this?"

It is you. They're right, of course. You have felt it all falling away, and it has not been an unpleasant sensation, this loosening of the tight-held things, this opening up of the hands.

Look, they're open.
They're empty.

Back to the medical profession, this time a
counsellor. Therapist. Whatever. Her name is long, and
her degrees are longer, and she is costing the family a
pretty penny. You know that there are several ways to
go here. Depression will get you pills. Acting out will
get you more therapy. Anarchy will get you...
"You know why you're here."
"I do?"
"Of course, you do. Why don't you tell me."
You smile at this deftless approach. Not so fast.
We're paying you the big bucks here.
A lot of sitting around. You wish you'd brought a
book or a deck of cards.
"You can remain mute, but you'll still have to stay
the entire session. I'm afraid your parents would insist."
She is not an evil therapist. She is merely a bored,
disinterested one, a woman with a career spent
listening to other people's problems. What does that do
to a person over time? you'd like to ask.
"They're concerned about you."
You shuffle your feet. "About my marks."
This is the opening the therapist has been waiting
for. "Not your marks, you."
And so it begins.
Of course, you're depressed. The only boy who ever
talked to you is dead. You're a loser at school. Your
artificial sister has to stick up for you, and she doesn't
even want to.
It's natural to feel depressed. But is it natural to have

a young man beaten to death? To have no one, not a single person, help him? To have no one caught? Is it natural to sit by yourself because no one wants to sit with you?

Dr. Millicent McCormack has no answers. That is not her job. She prods gently until the session is over.

"Until next time, then."

She does not rise or shake hands.

Not much happens in the next session, or the session after that. In the meantime, a parcel arrives, addressed to you. Annie Fournier carries it into the kitchen and drops it in front of you.

"Lovely parting gifts," she says.

You read the return address. The Ventners.

Your hands are trembling as you tear at the brown paper. Unfold the cloth. A cape. Black. The attached note reads:

Suzanne,

He wore it most of the time near the end. I can't look at it any more. Maybe you'd want it.

You stand up and wrap the cape around your shoulders. It flows down to your shoes. A magic cape.

"What's that?" Annie explodes in laughter.

You swirl slowly, the cape moving with you. Dar wore this, when he was magic.

"You look like a freakin' sideshow wizard!"

You put up the hood.

From then on you live in the cape. Your parents are frustrated beyond belief. They had thought the counselling sessions would make a difference, but now you parade around like a druid!

"You'll get expelled."

"I don't think so."

"You'll get picked on. You will. Why do you think…do you want to end up like that boy?"

There it is, then. Fear. Fear of you. Fear for you.

"It attracts the wrong kind of kids," your mother says in the kitchen.

You listening behind the door.

"She's going to wind up in trouble," your father agrees. He is having a tough time of it. His secret life is over. Amazingly, your mother is still unaware of the affair, which has ended badly, you believe. Doesn't your mother notice that he is home all the time now, that he mopes around the house?

Your mother doesn't, which is probably part of it all. Robert Cardinal has lost the other one and has only this happy family to sustain him: his wife, his adopted daughter and the freak in the black cape.

Suddenly, you feel sorry for your parents. This couldn't have been the game plan.

"What are we going to do with her?"

Tears now, from a mother who loves her wayward daughter. Motherhood such a disappointment after all.

You enter the kitchen. Surprised heads turn.

"I heard," you say, before they can ask. "I'm sorry. Really, I am."

Nothing to say.

Say nothing.

Monks did it. Nuns. Sealed themselves in walls.

Easy at school, where you are not known as an active participant. You are sure your teachers don't even notice the self-imposed discipline. There is no one to talk to at lunch anyway. There is no one to tell anything to.

And when you get the feeling again, when you see it, the back door of the bus is closing, but the girl is only halfway on; one hand has her schoolbooks, one hand is on the handrail. You see the girl's face, an expression somewhere between anticipation and dread, and the doors close on her. The bus takes off. She is dragged along the gritty street as the bus picks up speed, dragged, then she rolls over by the side of the road, and you can see her when they turn her ripped face skyward.

You witness this over and over and can now recognize the girl. She goes to your school. Fire Engine Sue wants to warn her, to do whatever it takes to get her to believe you. But you pull the hood up on your cape and greet the day in silence.

Therapy today.
"Tell me," the doctor says. Her mantra.
Tell her what?
When have they ever believed me?

Dear Mrs. Reidel,
It's grey outside, and there's a quiet rain falling. I'm working on a project about Egyptian death practices. It's cool and a bit gross. I think they had it wrong, but in such a cool way.

Ferg is in heaven by now. Kitty Heaven. Do you believe in a heaven for animals?

Of course, you'd probably know by now, one way or the other, so it wouldn't be about belief.

Everything here is belief. I don't know what I believe.
Belief. Faith.
"Faith, Hope and Love, and the greatest of these is Love."
They said that at Dar's funeral.

You have been right about your father. He comes in from the garage around midnight for a glass of water, and there he is in the living room in the dark.

You think he notices you. He sighs in your direction. You have to say something. "Maybe it's for the best."

Your voice startles him. He stares up at you with flustered comprehension on his face.

Yes, Father, I know.

"It's okay," you say, patting his head as if he's a child. "It'll be okay."

Your presentation at school goes better than expected. You have chosen to enact various Egyptian death rituals. In costume, you feel protected. Your silence is odd, but somehow appropriate, as you display photographs on the overhead projector, implements used to extract the brain through the nose. You work on the first-aid dummy, pretending to remove a sponge-rubber brain from its shiny plastic head. You proceed to wrap the dummy tightly in long linen cloths, sprinkling water on the material. You continue the ritual until the mummy is prepared for the sarcophagus. The class is actually interested. There is scattered applause.

The student in the long robes and strange eye makeup sits down.

Dear Mrs. Reidel,

I did it. The dummy is now a mummy.

We put it back in the closet as a mummy. There's gonna be a surprise next first-aid day.

I don't smell anything any more. I can't smell rain or grass. I don't like the city. You might like Mrs. Main's flowers, though. Not too shabby, you'd probably say.

Yours were nicer, though.

Your silver fingernails part your hair as you resume writing.

Annie might be in love. Hard to tell.

But she's weird about this new guy. She's too busy to crank my chain a lot. Always off with him. Doesn't bring him around much, though. She's no fool.

The feelings don't stop, despite your silence. The visions come more often now, three in a week. You have never been afraid of them, not like you are now. They are exhausting. How unfortunate that you have chosen not to talk to people.

"Dr. McCormack. Howdy."

She is still in a spin over the cape.

Your parents? When you think of them as parents, you are a very little girl, and you are holding on, all four of you together, and Carla is just walking. You love them, of course. But it is like standing by the tracks and loving the person in the crash.

The last vision was extreme. There was a child, a little boy with light brown hair. He was wearing a sweater, the old-fashioned kind. That is how you would have described it, though when you read the report in the paper, they said it was a Fair Isle pattern. You could see his sweet face, his trusting eyes that had never known real pain or fear, or worse. In your self-imposed world of silence, you can still hear his screams.

You tried to remove it from your mind. Over the years, you have found ways, tricks that make the images dull. But there is no way to stop the screams.

You don't like to read the paper but it arrives—plop —on your doorstep every day. You can't avoid the headlines or Annie's morbid lust for details.

"Do you see what they did to this kid?"

You can't stop seeing it.

"Apparently, we all need love," Dr. McCormack says, as though this has just occurred to her.

You wear the hood even in her office.

"Would you say that's a reasonable statement?"

Your fingernails are chipped from trying to shred the wood on your bedroom door.

"You need love, Suzanne."

The screaming finally stops, but only when the boy dies, again, in your eyes.

They are in the process of finding you love.

Your little suitcase, the one you packed to move to the city, is packed again.

"It's a group home, dear. You're not far, and it won't be for long, we hope. We just want you to get the help you need. You know, to cope."

Will you be able to take your journal? You have hidden it in the lining, but will you find a place, an empty classroom or an olive-coloured desk where you are going?

Annie hangs onto the banister on her way down to your basement room.

"Don't let anybody screw with you. You tell them. Tell them you've got a mean sister who's built like a tank, and she'll come sort them out."

Her foot is dangling between steps.

You smile.

"Well…" Annie says, then plants her foot on the step, turns on it, and heads back upstairs.

Laser Love

I do learn some things. How to smile when spoken to. How to answer questions.

Even when I don't know the answer.

We're hope fiends—me, Jule and Mark. We give one another signals with our eyes, and we know.

I've been reading about Kashmir. The place, not the wool. I found this book in the library reading room. In Kashmir, people are cold. They have these little portable fireboxes called kangri. They light them and put them beneath their robes, under their knees, when they sit. They sleep with them, too, although they have to balance them between their thighs, or they set their beds on fire. Women develop permanent purple marks on their inner thighs from holding their kangri close. I like it. People with fires beneath them, fires no one can see. Hold your kangri close.

Baxter and Scullion, Mark and Jule.

The Hope Fiends are in a special class with me because we're "special". All of us. Which kind of takes the "special" out of it, doesn't it?

I'm the Daughter of Doomsday. This is because they

119

make me tell about the things I sometimes see. The bad things that will happen.

-"Haven't you noticed, Suzanne, that the bad things always seem to happen to someone else? Why is that?"

-"You seem to have a lot of anger, Suzanne."

-"Show me my future."

-"Yeah, come on, Scrooge."

-"It wasn't Scrooge, it was the ghosts…"

-"Am I gonna marry a loser, or what?"

-"Yeah, are my pantyhose gonna run?"

The Daughter of Doomsday must answer when spoken to. House rules.

-"I see absolutely nothing in your future."

-"And mine?"

-"Nothing happens to you. Ever."

-"Me?"

-"Something horrible, but the good thing is, you never realize it."

The Hope Fiends meet in the yard. Climb the only tree, its generous branch wide and accommodating. I have three sesame snaps. They're sticky, even in the cold air, but we pull them apart with our fingernails. We watch the one-eyed squirrel wandering around the yard. Squirrels are not the brightest of souls. They never find half of what they hide. Just like us.

Mark swings down and picks up a fallen leaf. He climbs back up and twirls it in Jule's face so she goes cross-eyed. I think they love each other. They let me be with them. They want a lock on the future, they say.

Jule is skinny like me, but taller. She's a faded, almost paper-white colour, with pale grey eyes. She has

scars on her wrists, which she covers with leather
bracelets. She doesn't go anywhere without Mark.

Mark...he's good. He graffitis anything that doesn't
move, and one or two trucks that did move. The cop
car was his big mistake. He's leaning across Jule, his ear
to her breast, his hair loose and wild.

"I can hear the milk ocean."

Jule punches him.

I tell them about the fireboxes.

"Far out, but don't tell Monika."

I share a room with Monika, our resident firebug. It
hit me the first day we were together, the fire-starter
and Fire Engine Sue.

She's okay. She just has this thing for fires. She says
more boys do it than girls. Monika has a radio that gets
the short-wave, and she lets me listen to British radio
stations, which is how I get to hear T.Rex. Bolan has a
new single out in England. "Laser Love". It's good, but I
prefer the B-side, "Life's an Elevator".

"Life's an elevator," I say.

"So?" Jule.

"Life's a box with buttons and a cable?" Mark.

"Life's an elevator in a building with no floors." Me.

Journals are required here. But not secret ones. It's
harder than ever but, nevertheless... See, they like to go
over everything we write, every pearl of wisdom.

Mark is giving them old *Gilligan's Island* episodes,
only the names have been changed to protect
the...Gilligans?

"So the Professor says to Mr...Bowel..."

I told him *The Brady Bunch* would be more
convincing, but he's sticking with the castaways. Me, I

give them what they want.

"I am coming to terms with what I see as a burden I must carry." No, not carry. "Shoulder."

Personal deportment. Everything counts. How we handle ourselves.

"Gently, but firmly," Mark whispers. His eyes flash. I would be lost without the Hope Fiends.

Can't go home, not right now. The last time I was home was over half a year ago. Christmastime. It was bad. Better not to go at all than to see them so sad.

Annie's knee surgery is over, at least. She may even play again. But there were balloons bursting all over the place. Annie couldn't move around much, so I sat with her and we watched *The Price is Right* and *Laverne and Shirley*. At night we stayed up and watched her little portable TV. We looked weird in the flickering light. We laughed at how Johnny Carson's "Karnak" could predict the future.

My Christmas Treasure Trove:
-3 pairs thick wool socks
-1 plaid shirt (I'm a lumberjack...)
-a book about endurance (Annie wants to borrow it for her boyfriend)
-glitter and a kaleidoscope from Annie!

I brought home leatherwork. When Annie opened her gift and saw the belt, I could tell she was embarrassed. She was probably remembering how she used to tell Mom and Dad that I'd eventually "work my way up to leather-craft."

"I like working with leather. Really," I tried to assure her.

A belt for my father and a wallet for my mother.

At night, Annie asked me if I would sleep in her room, so I pulled out an air mattress. Her knee was bothering her. I could hear her shifting painfully. We lay there in the dark and she said, "So, what's it like? Are they all crazy?"

"You mean like me?"

Jule's thin jawline, her head down during group discussion; Monika's twitchy fingers.

I could hear Annie moving in the dark. "You're not nuts."

She wanted to know if I felt I was getting better.

"I talk more now."

"So? Allie Johnson talks all the time, and she's an idiot."

"Yeah. And she's your best friend, Annie."

"So?" She groaned as she moved her leg. "So, are there any cute teachers or therapists there?"

I laughed at that one. "Nope."

"Kill 'em off," Annie snorted. "Zap 'em with your laser vision!"

The very first time Annie had referred to the things I sometimes see.

"I don't control it."

"What a rip," she sighed. "You could have warned me about this." I could hear her patting the lump beneath the covers.

Annie fell asleep and left me in the dark, in my old house, looking out the window.

Jule wasn't allowed to go home back at Christmas. Her father's what got her into all of this. And Mark...well, he says he's from another planet where they don't celebrate peace and love by killing turkeys and stuffing the asses with bread. Jule's not bad, when she's here. She's doing okay. No more cutting herself. And she's got Mark, and he protects her.

DIRECT QUESTION FOR THE DAUGHTER OF DOOMSDAY

"Do you feel responsible for the deaths of your sister and your friend?"

All eyes on me. And then Mark's, and Jule's.

"Suzanne, surely you've had time to think about this. Is it still an issue for you?"

"All you need is love!" Mark shouts.

Eyes turn away from me.

"Mark? You want to say?"

"It's a Valentine's card I got once. It said:
'All you need is love; love is all around,
Like pennies from heaven, love drops without a sound.'"

"That's all very well, Mark, but..."

"Well, what do you suppose it *means?* Love drops? What the hell are love drops? And pennies make a lot of friggin' noise. And what do they mean by...?" Mark.

"I think love drops are these tear-shaped globules. Sort of sticky, I think." Jule.

Discussion diverted.

This past Valentine's Day, I got a card from Annie. Picture of a penguin in a toque, on an ice floe. It said, *"Bring me in out of the cold, baby."* I got thinking. The penguin would die. I know. I used to build penguin houses. Annie scribbled inside the card, "Zap 'em with your X-ray eyes."

Yeah, like Bowie's "Moonage Daydream", from the *Ziggy Stardust* album. I definitely feel like I'm freaking out sometimes. I keep dreaming of other places. Tibet. England—one ticket to Middle Earth, or the Lake District, or a ride on that cool new Concorde from Paris to New York. A trek to the Indies. A Himalayan climb. I'll sit at night, my kangri between my knees, my whole body hunched around it, my little light hidden but burning, warming me, keeping me safe while the snow falls all night on my shoulders.

<u>July, 1977</u>

Monika is gone. She took off one afternoon and went on a spree. She lasted a few good days, then I heard she'd been picked up for trying to light a Tim Hortons. I don't know where she is. But I have my own room for now. I put up Dar's Bolan posters. Dar was right. I am lucky. My hair is the same as Bolan's. Annie sent me a Bowie poster as well. He and Bolan are friends.

I was sitting in the TV room when I heard about Monika's capture. Young Adolf, the admin clerk, came in, and you could tell he just couldn't wait to gush out the good news. As he was talking, the Chiffon margarine commercial came on the screen and said, "It's not nice to fool Mother Nature." Between that and Eric Carmen droning, "All by Myself" down the hall, I thought I'd finally arrived.

Jule is sick with a bad tooth. I found Mark.

"Wanna go for a walk?"

He was a bit spacey today, missing Jule.

"Sure," he shrugged.

"Let's get out of here."

We walked downtown. It's a long walk. Must have taken us about an hour and a half. But it was good to be out, on the side of the road.

"You want to hitch?" he'd asked. I looked at us. His pony-tailed hair, my dust-covered pants. Our goofy faces.

"Let's walk."

"Because?"

"Because we can."

Not like Crazy Eugene. He's a mess. Don't know what happened to him, but he's in a wheelchair now, and we never see him. I hear he's going to be transferred.

We walked.

It was good to be downtown again. We pooled our resources—six bucks and change. Bought some jasmine tea and a piece of cake to split. We could have given it all to the Hare Krishnas, who were passing out plates of free food. The rice was saffrony, but I didn't know what the other stuff was. And it looked so dry and dusty. I hate their outfits, and I'd look insane with their haircut. But they were playing music and chanting, and it was okay.

There was a dance club nearby, but without money, what was the point? We sat in the train station for a while, listening to destinations.

"When I was a kid," Mark said, and it occurred to me that I've never thought of him that way, "every year we'd go west to visit relatives. My whole family would take the train, and they'd play cards and read books and get bored and stuff. My little sister used to go to the snack bar about ten times an hour. I used to look out the window. Especially at night, when everyone was sleeping in their bunks…berths, whatever you call them. The lights would be out, and I'd pull up the heavy blinds, the ones that covered the whole long window, and I'd watch the country go by."

"Must have been weird."

"It was fantastic. Lying in your bed, and then just turning your face and watching the world move across the length of your body, like it was imprinting itself onto you."

"Or you onto it, I guess."

He looked at me. "Yeah. It was great."

I tried to imagine.

Then he told me how he'd secretly wish he could get out in the middle of nowhere, a passing field, and just walk through the grass in the moonlight.

I didn't tell him, but I knew exactly what he meant.

He said he saw a couple of deer once, and he wanted to follow them up the clearing into the bush.

So I kissed him. I just leaned in and kissed him, then pulled away.

He sat there.

I felt horrible. I opened my mouth to say…

He stopped me. Not to kiss me back. "Funny how when people are in train stations, they kiss all the time."

People kiss all the time.

I walked the rest of the day with that one.

•

A small purple light moving along a dark street.
Twinkles. There is a bridge ahead, arced like a rainbow.
Cars are always kissing the pavement, the cobblestones,
and purple glows, even over the bridge. Ahead, more
road. But for the tiny purple car leaving the surface, the
fence is insubstantial, a figment, a fragment. The tree
reaches up to embrace the flying lights.

•

I can't get it out of my head. Metal in my mouth.

•

"Suzanne, we need to discuss what happened last night.
Look at you. Why did you do that to your face?"

Face? My...

The mirror is round, like a beauty queen's, but the
face has red lines.

"You clawed your face, Suzanne. Why?"

Eyes. Eyes always protect themselves. Cause all the
problems, then shut tight and let the face take it.

"You ran screaming down the hall with your face
bloody. Could you tell me what's going on?"

Stings. The lines on my face. Bizzaro Superman in the
old comic books. Parallel-universe Superman. The lines,
like someone licking you with a pointed steel tongue.

"You were really doing well. Has something upset
you? What happened yesterday?"

"Never gonna get old."

"What? What does that mean, Suzanne? Wait, here's
Dr. Harvey. I called him in."

Harvey. Like the giant pookah Jimmy Stewart was friends with in that old black and white movie. One of my father's favourites.

"Hello, Suzanne. It's been a while since we talked. Are you comfortable, or would you like to sit somewhere else?"

Jimmy Stewart was Elwood P. Dowd. He had a huge invisible rabbit named Harvey.

"I see something has upset you. Do you want to talk about it? I'll clear everyone else out, and you can just talk to me, okay?"

We are alone, me and the giant pookah. Hey, I can see him, Elwood! I knew he existed, even though we only got to see him at the end of the movie.

"I heard you were in the city yesterday. How was that?"

Cars. Noise.

"Traffic."

"Yes, that's why I'm a little late, in fact. Quite a change from here. You went in with young Baxter, isn't that right?"

"Mark, yeah."

"Everything was okay? What did you do with yourselves?"

I keep my head down. The blood rushes to the stinging red lines.

"Suzanne?"

"I saw something."

Pages flipping in a file. Pages and pages of Suzanne Cardinal.

"Another episode? Says here you haven't had one since…why, you've been doing well, Suzanne. So. An episode. Tell me about it."

Close my eyes, but it's still there, tattooed there, sharp tongues with blades have etched it good.

"Cars."

"Did the traffic bother you? Tell me."

"Someone is going to die. In a car."

"Another premonition," he notes on the page. "Although, Suzanne, it's hardly a stretch to predict that."

Daughter of Doomsday.

But this time. You can't stand it this time.

Bolan.

Hands to your face to keep out the vision of the purple car careening into the ancient tree. The tree rises, Bolan breathes it in, branch and sinew. Bark kisses his sweet, sweet face.

Now my face is rough like bark.

I am under observation. I haven't seen Mark or Jule. I have to get to a phone. I have to write a letter. They won't let me go back to my room. I need paper.

"I need a phone."

"Not right now, Suzanne."

I need to warn him.

"I have to call my parents…please."

Much consultation. By afternoon I can call.

"Yeah?"

Annie.

"Thank God, Annie. It's me."

"Laser Babe. Hey, I'll get…"

"No! No. Annie, I need to talk to you."

Annie Fournier.

"What do you want with me?"

"Annie, you have to get me out."

"Whoa. You know I can't do that. That's between you and Mom and Dad."

"I need numbers. I need to contact him."

"What...hey, spaz, what's going on?"

"He's going to die."

"Who?"

"Bolan."

I can hear it in her voice before she even speaks.

"Annie, I saw. He's going to die."

"Hot flash, we're all going to die! Look, this is crazy fan shit. I told you about that groupie crap..."

"Annie, please!"

.

I'm in Jule's room. She's playing Bowie. "Ziggy Stardust". I tell her what I saw. She asks me if there's any chance I could be wrong. "I'm wrong about a lot of stuff," she tries, offering up her father, her partial suicides.

Then she comes over and holds my hands, looking into the palms as if she can find the answer there.

"Send a telegram to his studio in England."

I look into her tired eyes.

"You know, like when the *Titanic* was sinking."

"What?"

"A telegram. 'Telegram Sam.'"

She puts Bolan's *Slider* album on the turntable and plays me "Telegram Sam."

Next day Annie comes, and we drive downtown. Annie is playing ball again and is almost all the way back with her knee, though she doesn't know how the

131

delay will affect her scholarship.

"I had a long talk with Mom and Dad last night. They said they were sorry you're unhappy."

"I'm not unhappy."

"They were sad to hear that you still get your spells."

"I don't get spells."

Annie has taken desperate instruction well and has the scribbled address of the EMI office in London.

"I don't know if it's the right one. I don't know if he's with them now."

"Neither do I," I say.

I've never sent a telegram. "Telegram Sam" is playing in my head as I try to think of what to say.

MARC BOLAN STOP DANGER DON'T GET IN PURPLE CAR STOP

ACCIDENT TREE STOP

"Whoever gets this is going to think it came from a loony," Annie says, reading over my shoulder.

"It did." I count the words. Does it make sense?

Annie pays for it. I don't know what she pays. I'm cold and tired. She drives me to a greasy spoon and forces me to sit with a burger. I just want to lie down.

"Doesn't help that you've messed your face up so you look like a freak, you know."

She's the one who stares down the hamburger guy.

"You're pretty much a wreck, you know that? I thought you were doing better there."

Annie's dipping her fries in my ketchup.

"I was. Am. I have friends."

"I didn't see anybody I'd want to call a friend."

"You don't know. I have friends there."

"Mom and Dad are hoping you'll be able to come

home in a couple of months. They've moved your room back up and painted it."

"What about your exercise room?"

"Ah, I do some weights in the basement, but the rest of the time I'm at the gym or rehab."

The radio station is playing ABBA.

Annie sucks up the last of her drink.

"So, how come Bolan hasn't made it big here? I mean, if he's so good."

He's the 20th Century Boy. He's the Wizard. He sings to the Metal Guru.

"He had, what, one hit here? Two?"

ABBA continues to bleat. My head hurts.

"Annie, I need to go back now."

She leaves me at the gate. She doesn't want to say much, I can tell. I open the door, but then I lean over and squeeze her upper arm. Hard as a rock.

"Thank you."

"Yeah, go on. No one's gonna pay attention to it, you know. The telegram? Just thought you should know that."

I have tears in my eyes, but I smile at Annie Fournier. I am beginning to figure that much out.

I go right to my room. Bolan looks down at me from the wall. I think of Dar Ventner, which I haven't done in a while. He'd be almost twenty now, with a job and a place of his own. He'd be in a band, maybe, and in love with a young beauty. The beauty would be a boy like him, long-fingered and lost, and they would walk entwined.

Mark Baxter and Jule Scullion, the Hope Fiends, come by. I tell them about the telegram and Annie.

"It's something," Jule says.

"It's not enough," I say, as Mark picked at the veneer on my bureau.

"I heard Bowie might be coming for a concert."

"Wow! When?"

"Not sure. It's still a rumour."

"If he comes, we go, right?"

Mark turns and puts his arms out for us. "Of course."

We are lying on the bed, me, Jule and Mark. We live in each other's minds now.

<u>August, 1977</u>

I have been writing him letters, two or three a week. They like to monitor everything here, and I just know what they'd say, so I get Jimmy, the groundskeeper, to mail them for me. Jimmy's willing to do it if I sit on his lap out around back of the toolshed. I don't care.

Dear Marc Bolan,

Did you receive my telegram? Are you there? It's like you said, "Life's a Gas."

You know, that you want it to last? I know you have a baby now, a little boy.

You have to be careful. Don't go in any cars. Stay away from cars.

Sincerely,
Suzanne Cardinal

•

Dear Marc Bolan,

*Please. I saw it again last night. Somewhere in
London. Please.*
Sue

•

Dear Bolan,
*Almost morning. So so late. So early. Can you hear
me? It will be late,*
And early, in the car. You love cars. All your songs—
*Cadillacs, Jeepsters, Jaguars, hubcapped-diamond-star-
halos. Do you know it, too? Can you*
See what I see?
Fire Engine Sue

•

I'm leaving the home. It doesn't matter, now that Mark
and Jule are going. They'll try living together. I don't
know what I'll do.

Out on the wide tree branch. Jimmy has mowed the
grass, and the place is quiet now. Just this tree. It's big
and broad like the tree in the dream. My legs dangle
down from the branch.

"There she is."

They run to me, the Hope Fiends.

They'll be going soon.

"Why are you hiding from us?"

Long afternoons with the friends I find in books.

"Busy."

"Too busy for us?" Mark's idea of busy is to graffiti a
large wall in a short period of time.

135

"We wondered, see, because the rent for the place I got is hefty for just me and Jule. I can get work at my cousin's restaurant. Jule thinks she can work. But, well, we need you."

"My money?" My feet are heavy.

"No, you, idiot. We need you."

Jule's pale wolf eyes looking up into mine.

"Try it," she said. Her smile is better since they fixed her tooth.

Three in a tree, colourful legs like those of a giant spider, the far side of the toolshed covered in graffiti.

•

I have a new home. I have a bowl of short-stemmed orange and yellow nameless flowers in a bowl on the table. The curtains are yellow and blue. Jule and Mark (and sometimes me) sleep in the big room off the living-room. I have my own little room that is by itself near the back balcony. It's green like eyes. I try to make the room like a formal tea room in *The Book of Tea*. I like the plainness. But I just can't take down the posters.

I make rice. Pancakes. Jasmine tea.

I have wind-chimes and a dreamcatcher.

I told Annie to come by and see it. She stopped in on her way from practice. Knocked on the door. When I opened it, she seemed almost shy. I think she was afraid Mark and Jule would be there, three crazies instead of one.

"I'm alone. Come on in."

Annie stepped through the door and looked around. There was a baking failure on top of the stove, but other than that the place didn't look too messy.

"Pretty plain. What's the word? Spartan."

She stood in the middle of the living room and made it look small.

"We don't have a lot of stuff."

"Yeah," she nodded. "Cool."

I made some tea. Camomile. Annie hates jasmine tea.

"Sorry. The cake is a write-off."

"Can't eat it anyway. Team diet."

We didn't have much to talk about, we never do, but I knew she wanted to see how I was doing. She and my parents.

"You're liking it here, aren't you?"

It's like she was seeing me for the first time. I kept thinking of the sticker on the mailbox: Baxter, Scullion, Cardinal.

I have to work for this. I make jewellery and sell it down at the co-op. I also put in my hours there to get cheaper food. Near the co-op, there's this new club. It's kind of a punk bar, pretty seedy, but we're all gonna go there soon. Jule traded in her glitter for black eyeliner. She already has the pale face. She's okay about everything; when I'm close with Mark, when I'm close with her. We're all we have.

"Don't forget about school." Annie. This from Annie?

"You'll want to go back. You're smart, way smarter than I am."

"I can't play ball."

I wear glitter on my cheekbones and eyes, and I put glitter down my front, in case anyone wants to look. I turn on my music, and the living room is my world. I see the purple car. I see it all the time.

September 1977

No school for me this year. Have to work and dance and love my friends. The Hope Fiends have taken over. We go to the club and listen to the three-chord songs. I like the anger and energy but miss the music. We don't dance at the punk bar, but I found another place where they play beautiful music. It's dark and smoky, but I can flash my shiny eyes.

Dear Bolan,
It's small and purple. The road is dark and stretches out like the backbone of a dragon. You rise up on the dragon and then you, you fall back...

Husha, husha
All fall down.
Carla and Dar and Mrs. Reidel in the same cemetery in the same town. I bury all my loves there.

Sold three bracelets and a necklace today. This one woman wanted jade, but she settled for tiger-eye. How can you settle for a completely different thing? Not that I'm complaining.

My mother got my number from Annie Fournier. So she called. Told me I was wasting my life and my talent.

Which would that be? The one where I see things and nobody believes me?

"You could go on and get a degree. You were good in everything when you were young."

They don't give degrees in finger painting.

I'm reading. Castenada, Buddhist texts, Nathaniel Hawthorne. Jule turned me on to him—strange guy. There's a lot of people like that out there, people who are talking from different times, but talking right to me. Laurence Sterne, after you get over the goofy language. I like *Tristram Shandy*. Sterne was probably a cool guy to hang around with.

Most of the writers are dead. But I still hear them. Maybe we're haunted; maybe we all have "talents", as my mother calls them. I like reading. Jule reads a couple of books a week, when she's feeling well. Mark would rather go out and find a deserted building somewhere. He hates blank walls.

We dance.

"That's not a profession unless you study dance and make it a profession."

We dance and are in perfect harmony.

"Nobody watches you. No one would pay to watch you dance."

It's like music. It comes out of you. What you do with it is your choice, but it will not be denied.

"A freaking artist," Annie said when I tried to explain. "What are you gonna do with that?"

"Dance. Starve."

She scowled.

"Annie, I can't play ball."

Always shuts her up. It is, for her, the thing. She would be lost without it, as she was when her knee was healing. She left me ten dollars on the kitchen table.

When Jule and Mark came home, we went out for pizza. That started our discussion, and our first big fight since we've been living together. I think someone is jealous, but I can't tell who. I just stayed in my little green room in the back, just me and Bolan, who watched me from the wall. The tea room should have one object on which to focus.

Bolan? Or me?

I woke up ice-cold. I couldn't see anything except the car and the oak tree. I stumbled out of bed and hit the floor, scrambled over to the window and threw it open. The air was cold, but not as cold as me.

Breathe in the whole night sky.

Hold. Hold it in. If only I could hold it all in.

Dinner at my parents' place. Labour Day.

"Which might mean something if some people were working."

Annie had already moved into her university dorm and was just home for the weekend. She and I sat up late watching *Saturday Night Live*. Sunday dinner, then Annie would be heading back on Monday, so they pulled out all the stops—ham, potatoes (hot, plus cold potato salad), two other salads, peas and a strawberry-rhubarb crumble for dessert on top of the pumpkin pie.

"You eat like a fly, Suzanne."

I eat shit?

"Robert, look at her, she's skin and bones. I don't think she's eating over there."

My father glanced my way but couldn't meet my eyes. He's relinquished me.

My mother packed leftover food into pie plates and wrapped them up. She stuffed them into a hideous phentex bag and insisted that I take it with me. When I went to the door, Annie flashed me a peace sign.

"Be careful. Watch what you watch," she said.

My mother hugged me. In her arms, I could tell that she was right. I was skin and bones. She made a noise in her throat, and I knew it meant she loved me. Same as the hand on my back that was my father's push.

They wanted to drive me back, but I told them the bus was quicker. It isn't, not on a Sunday. I stood a block and a half away at the stop, looking over my former neighbourhood. The bench was graffiti-rich. Mark would have been impressed with our smug little enclave.

The bus came, and I sat halfway back on the right side, warm food in my lap, watching the houses drive away from my window.

September 16, 1977

Marc Bolan, British glam-rock superstar, television star, and leader of the band T.Rex, was killed early this morning in a car crash in southwest London. Bolan was travelling in a purple Mini along with his girlfriend, Gloria Jones. The single-vehicle accident occurred when the car, which was travelling on Queen's Ride at the southern edge of Barnes Common, crossed over a bridge and left the road, going through a fence and hitting a tree. Jones, the driver, was injured in the crash. Bolan died instantly. Marc Bolan leaves behind both Jones and their two-year-old son, Rolan.

"I heard it on the BBC earlier today. I didn't know how to tell you."

Jule's hands are on my head.

"I'm sorry. I'm so sorry."

Mark rocking me back and forth.

He goes out and scours the newspapers. He has the radio on in the bedroom. They're in my room now, and Bolan is staring at them too.

"You were right. Right down to the colour and make of the car," Mark marvels. He's been listening to broadcasts on shortwave. "Can't get a lot of information. All they want to talk about is some opera singer, this Maria Callas chick. She just croaked in Paris, and they keep laying on her music. But over in England, man, it's Bolan."

I step out onto the balcony. I can hear industrial carpet cleaners from the office building next door. Jule holds my arm, but I pull free.

August 1977

What was Marc Bolan's last hit?
A tree.

A tree. So they are saying. I hate fans.

We have a memorial service, me, Jule and Mark. We play music, and we dance. I light a candle and say a prayer, which I've hardly done since Carla. I go up on the mountain overlooking the city. The hive buzzes below, all of them scurrying. See, I've already prayed and cried and cursed. I broke the mystery of that a long time ago.

We read in a paper that Bowie went to his funeral. So did Rod Stewart and Elton John. Annie was right about Elton John; he's okay. Bolan's ashes are under a rosebush in the Keats Rose Bed, in a place called Golders Green.

<u>Still August 1977</u>

I didn't know much about Keats. He's a poet, and I'm not afraid of libraries, so I went and got a collection and started reading. I found this:

> ...*When I behold, upon night's starred face,*
> *Huge cloudy symbols of a high romance,*
> *And think that I may never live to trace*
> *Their shadows, with the magic hand of chance;*
> *And when I feel, fair creature of an hour,*
> *That I shall never look upon thee more,*
> *Never have relish in the faery power*
> *Of unreflecting love!—then on the shore*
> *Of the wide world I stand alone, and think*
> *Till love and fame to nothingness do sink.*

And so ends my career as Cassandra, resident seer, Daughter of Doomsday. If they want to medicate me, they can go ahead. If they want me to ignore it, I will. I'll stop listening to what my heart tells me, what I see in my eyes.

Look around you. Other people do it. Other people do it all the time.

Executive Summary

1981-1992

Suzanne Cardinal glanced at her watch. Fifteen minutes to go. A quarter of an hour sitting and toting up numbers alongside old Cliffy who, any moment now, would start apologizing to the filing cabinet for closing the drawer too hard. Cliff was unaware that he talked to inanimate objects. Or maybe it was all the same to him—people, things, objects in the path of his downcast eyes. Shoes or casters, it didn't matter much to Cliffy.

She had been here almost two years. Hard to believe. She should be grateful to Aunt Sophie for pulling a few strings from her working years. It was Sophie who had got Suzanne the interview, not Suzanne's non-existent resumé. At least she'd completed high school, although she wondered if anyone ever really counted those night school certificates. But that gap in time. People were always suspicious when it came to unaccountable lapses. She could have been doing foreign aid. She could have been in prison or have had a baby. She could have been crazy.

Aunt Sophie had suggested a haircut, which Suzanne declined, willing, instead, to wrap her small tight curls and frizzy ringlets in elastics, creating a severe-looking bun on her head. The effect was Asian, this petite woman, her hair in a topknot, her clothes tailored and plain.

So plain. Aunt Sophie called Adele, who called Suzanne.

"What did you wear when you went to see her before the interview?"

"I don't know. A dress. No, a jumper."

"She said you looked like a pent-up nun."

Her mother trod carefully, though, as it was generally agreed that the demented nun was better than the magic sparkling nymph.

"Do you have anything a bit more springy?"

"What, like Spandex?"

A sigh that almost blew out her eardrum.

"Spring-*like*. Bright. But not too bright. You know, pretty, floral."

Pastel.

The interview had been strange. Why did she want to work for an insurance company?

Uhm…her aunt had worked there? She needed a job? Food?

She mumbled something about helping people in their time of need, which seemed to be the right answer. She started the following week and had been here almost two years.

She progressed, however, from walking papers from desk to desk for signatures to assisting agents and underwriters. She was taking courses at night. Accounting on Mondays, with a business admin option the following term. She did French. And poetry. Her boss, Mr. Forten, who had taken an undetermined interest in her, failed to see how poetry worked into the mix.

"Roses are red,
Violets are blue,
Don't pay your premium?
Not much I can do."

When Mr. Forten smiled, his broken left canine was visible. He was married to the pinched-looking woman in the photo on his desk. Two truly unattractive children stared defiantly from the portrait, the girl looking like she would powder your bones.

Two years. It had been four since she'd bolted from the group home and lived for a short time with friends. A lifetime ago. She hardly ever thought about that time. Her friends had left to travel. Annie had moved her in with some of Annie's friends, but that hadn't worked. Finally, she'd found a bachelor apartment with the world's tiniest fridge and stove.

"You'll have to cook your chicken in pieces," Annie laughed.

But it wasn't the smallest stove. A kangri was smaller. It would fit between her thighs. She took the apartment and stopped thinking about kangris and India.

Besides, there was always Mr. Forten to keep her on the right path. Suzanne's boss lived and breathed insurance. He was always talking about risk and probability, term insurance, life insurance. He advised people to take this or that package to maximize their returns.

Suzanne had no insurance. If she fell, she fell. If she died, well, she didn't imagine it would make too big a difference to the universal consciousness. Mr. Forten no doubt sensed her ambivalence, which was why he pelted her with books and articles.

"There's a disability seminar on this weekend. I may take it in. You should come."

Suzanne imagined a room filled with people of various disabilities, the seminar leader droning on to the deaf people, his slide shows flashing across the retinas of the blind. She imagined Mr. Forten's bunchy underpants and his skinny legs.

"Sorry. I'm busy."

1984   Annie Fournier's Wedding, July 17

The dress was ready. It had been a long-standing joke that Suzanne could not sew. And it was true—she could not sew worth a damn. But her afternoons making beaded jewellery with Jule and Mark had made her more than proficient at sewing on the several thousand crystal beads that now adorned Annie Fournier's gown. The result was impressive—Annie's tall frame enwrapped in white matte silk, the beads in a non-discernable pattern down the front of the dress. Suzanne placed the star clusters there: nebula swirls, galaxies of dust and light on the bodice. It was, in its own way, stunning, and it broke up the traditional look of the dress.

Annie was taken with it immediately. "It came out even better than you said."

Suzanne was examining each bead as the dress moulded itself around Annie.

"Really, thanks, Sue. This is fabulous. I don't know how you found the time."

Suzanne fiddled with the hem in the back. Time?
Time was like tea. You could always make more.

"Mom really wishes you'd be in the wedding party.
So do I…"

Suzanne stood and faced Annie. They both knew
that her hard work on the dress was in lieu of her being
forced to be a bridesmaid and to stand in a summer-
sweet pale green dress. Annie had spared her that.

"Okay," Annie conceded without Suzanne having
spoken a word.

Annie Fournier was marrying Ty Robertson, a
football player turned entrepreneur. He owned two
upscale sports clothing stores in Toronto and Ottawa
and was preparing to open a third in Vancouver.

"So, what about your guest?"

Suzanne knew that the question emanated from
Annie, but she could also hear her mother's voice
behind it.

"He'll be there."

"That's all you have to say? Come on, girl. How long
have you been seeing him?"

Eldon Dowland, graphic designer, was hardly a full-
time concern. He made that clear early on. He had his
work, his friends, and his hangers-on. She wasn't sure
where that put her. She could expect the unexpected,
she was told.

"Not long. A while."

They saw each other twice a week, once for dinner
and once, primarily, for sex. She did not know what he
did with his other evenings.

"Is he hot?" Annie asked, a woman in a wedding
dress and flip-flops.

149

"Yeah," Suzanne said. "Yes, he is very, very hot."

It was his charm that had attracted her. He could make you want him if he wanted to. Or perhaps it was his narcissism, a man in love with his own smile, his own body. It was like watching a movie about him. She could star in it a couple of days a week as a bit player. Contract player? An *extra*? He was prettier, more beautiful, than she was. His naked body, very much a dancer's form, was the perfect complement to the wonderfully arranged bones of his face. She liked to run her hands up and down his chest and torso, outlining him in her atoms.

On the wedding day, it did not rain, but it was hot and muggy. Adele was worried about bugs in the punch, salmonella in the cream toppings, this despite the caterer's assurances. The outdoor garden they had rented was well-appointed, with trellises, bowers, canopies and tables. White and pale pink flowers with green ferns abounded, complementing the pale green of the bridesmaids' dresses. A couple of Suzanne's former teammates looked decidedly uncomfortable in the high-waisted gowns. Suzanne was staring at the dresses when Eldon returned with their drinks.

"Well, that's over," he said, as if it had been particularly arduous.

"I thought it was nice."

"Nice? Oh, yes, well, we must say it was nice."

It was moving, actually, to see her father walk Annie down the grassy aisle. Annie looked serene, her hair upswept, the galaxies shifting on her dress as she stepped forward.

Suzanne's mother sniffled throughout the ceremony

and once even reached over and squeezed Suzanne's hand. The father of the bride beamed at his tall, shining daughter.

"When can we leave?" Eldon asked under his breath.

She was about to answer when she was accosted by Aunt Sophie, who had been toasting the bride and groom with vigor.

"I hear you're up for a promotion," she gushed.

"Sorry?"

"At work. Your promotion."

Did she still have her ear to the ground over there?

"I don't know. I'm taking courses at night. I also took one through the company."

"That's wonderful!" Aunt Sophie gestured dramatically, sending a tidal wave of champagne across the grass.

"Whoops! That's for the gods, then. Libations to the gods!"

Eldon made an almost imperceptible sound.

Annie threw the bouquet and Katherine, the maid of honour, caught it. Suzanne's mother cried on her husband's shoulder. Suzanne could tell that her father was looking her way. They hadn't talked. Her father was looking at Suzanne and Eldon. Did he see a couple there?

Eldon went to retrieve the car, parked in the grass at the end of a long driveway. Three other cars had to be moved before he could get his to the road.

"Let's just get out of here," he said, teeth gritted into a smile, "before I kill someone."

People waved them out of the driveway, and they were on their way. Clinical silence ensued, quieter than church, or a pelvic exam.

"You could have been nicer," Suzanne said at last.

His eyes were on the road.

"You could…"

"To whom? Drunk Aunt Sophie or your zombie father?"

"To my sister. It was her wedding day."

"Won't be her last."

She stared at his jawline, at the single pockmark he was always trying to hide.

"See what I mean, Eldon?"

"Sorry. Congratulations, and may she and that fat footballer live forever."

She hadn't been paying attention, she guessed. She hadn't noticed. This man was done with her. He just hadn't gotten around to telling her yet.

1986

Tuesday was the day it all changed. A Tuesday afternoon.

Suzanne had finished typing up notes; she had run telephone interference for Mr. Forten; she had filed policies.

Cliffy was muttering to the water cooler.

The elevator door opened, and a young couple stepped off. The woman's shoes were the kind Suzanne favoured, flat-soled, brown soft leather. The woman had a protective hand across her prominent stomach. Mother-to-be. Mr. Forten loved them. If there was anyone who craved security, it was a new parental unit. The husband wore a casual jacket and sweater.

These would be the Grahams. Mr. Forten had been priming them with options, all kinds of bells and whistles that would not pay off for years. He was really pushing the extra health insurance, guilting the soon-to-be father into higher coverage.

Suzanne greeted them and shook hands with the woman. She was supposed to escort them to Mr. Forten's office, but when she touched the man's hand, she froze. She was staring at a dead man. The vision ripped by her eyes so quickly, she barely had time to register it. The way his brown hair was perfect…but the bruise-like blue mark where the electricity passed through him.

She looked down at the papers in her hands. *Electrician.*

The young woman sat with a sigh. The husband smiled and went to the cooler to get her some water, returning to place it gently in her hands. His own hands so sure, so in control.

Suzanne's head was pounding. "You…" she shouted, startling the couple. "Uh…sorry. When are you due?"

"A month," the woman sighed again. "The home stretch is getting a little hard."

"Are you comfortable? I'm sure Mr. Forten will be right with you. I just have to go…photocopy something."

She raced out of the office and into the hall, poring over the notes. Mr. Forten was about to sign them up for long-term, future payoffs, payoffs they would need a lot sooner.

Composing herself, she walked determinedly back to Mr. Forten's office and closed the door. Within the fifteen minutes it took her boss to park his car and ascend the elevator, Suzanne had convinced the Grahams to go for the policy with the high death benefits. The man was young, in excellent health. There would be no problem getting reasonably-priced coverage.

The Grahams were cowed by Mr. Forten's counter-arguments but stuck with Suzanne's suggestion. Mr. Forten gave her a glance that said she might be back sharpening pencils any day now.

But as she fell asleep that night, she thought about Lorrie Graham and her little infant. They would be alone, but they would not be destitute. She thought about her final handshake with Lloyd Graham. He would be dead soon, she thought, as she rolled over and closed her eyes.

So it began again. She woke up three nights after the Grahams, shivering and gasping for air. Someone was going to drown. Who? She could see the body moving inside the car; she couldn't tell if it was a man or a woman. A face filmed by the window, eyes wide. Suzanne shook herself awake, went into the kitchen and made some peppermint tea.

Why now, after years of relative peace? She had actually laughed her way through 1984, the year of Orwellian revenge. He was wrong. Maybe she'd been wrong as well. Medication, meditation, mysticism, counselling. Maybe all she'd needed was the right fix.

She could sense no sudden shift in her situation. She had followed Mr. Forten's lead and was now drawing up insurance policies. She was going to dinner with Mr. Forten once a week to cheer him up since his divorce. She was dating, until recently, a Geological Survey researcher. She was minding Annie's baby any chance she got.

Little Zara was like her mother, all arms and legs.

Suzanne watched her parents hold the infant and saw them, briefly, as they were so long ago. Her father was building Zara a cradle for her dolls, just as he had for Suzanne. There was promise of a telescope somewhere down the line. Her mother was buying children's recordings and soft cloth books. Both of her parents sat together on the couch now, revelling in the grandchild.

And there it was again, her father's smile, that crooked, slightly shy acknowledgement of grace. Her mother looked years younger and was herself softer as she held the cloth books to the baby and pointed at the outlines. The baby, too young to know the profound effect she was having, gurgled or slept.

When the child was first born, Annie had looked at it with a mixture of wonder and fear. Suzanne knew better than to ask whether it had been planned. She knew that Annie had wanted to train for a few years after her marriage. Nobody said anything. They all wordlessly worshipped at the crib.

1988

"And how can we be of assistance to you today?" the insurance agent says, seeing to the client's immediate comfort. A pitcher of water and drinking glasses are on the table, as is a box of kleenex.

They want peace of mind, security. They want never to grow old or get sick, to stay close and tight and perfect. And when the "eventuality" happens, they want to keep a hand in from beyond the grave: a scholarship, a trust fund. Something recent, as yet unspoken, has shaken them. A parent dying? A brush with cancer? A home invasion?

Can she make it all go away? Can she give them back their innocence?

Fire Engine Sue will help us through.

She looks upon them kindly; there is such kindness in her face, they will later say. She assures them that they need not worry. Their insurance coverage is fine. They will live long lives.

What kind of company doesn't push its product? They are confused and momentarily suspicious, yet the woman is so calm. Whatever inside information she has she is certainly confident of its authenticity. They should be so lucky in their own lives.

The agent tells them that they have a lucky life. She notes their three children and the joy the little ones bring to their existence. And, they swear, they are blinking back tears by the time they leave the office. They wish they could thank Ms Cardinal in some way, especially considering they did not purchase a policy package. They are grateful, thankful, for the meeting and wave to her from the elevator.

.

Suzanne was dreaming through the accounting class, where the instructor was elaborating on accruals. People in front were scribbling notes. Something Mr. Forten said that morning came back to her. He was referring to a recent Royal Bank promotion of someone he had known in his university days. "A real toad, if you don't mind my saying." Then he was grousing about fairness and the universe, and he said that the whole thing was a rip-off.

Suzanne had smiled at the incongruity of these words emerging from Mr. Forten's mouth. And she found herself remembering the T.Rex song, "Rip-Off". Dancing to the saxophone, to the bongo beat. How Jule had insisted that they dance in the nude, just like in the song, Jule and Mark and Suzanne down at the park with the tramps. The memory was returned to the vault, but her foot tapped the metal leg of the lecture hall desk.

.

Mr. Forten played with the celery stalk in his Caesar. Sometimes it appeared to be a sinking barge, other times a long, slender spoon.

"So," he crunched. Now it was low-cal food. "Is something wrong?"

Suzanne shifted on the fake petit-point cushion. "Wrong?"

"With you. Are you having any difficulties? Because I've noticed a drop in your productivity. That is, new clients. That is, implementation of policies. You're down."

"I am?"

"You know you are. What's going on?"

The Thompsons didn't need the big policy. She could tell they were going to be okay. The Listers would need long-term disability. In fact, they were already beginning to make use of it. She saw Mrs. Lister in a hospital bed, a port in her arm and an intravenous dip attached. The Listers had come in for insurance for their college-aged son. Suzanne had convinced them to go for the disability insurance.

"I've signed up new people."

"You sure have. I've been going over your accounts. You've had a lot of people walk out without signing, but the ones who have stayed are taking us to the cleaners!"

"What? Like Mr. Graham? He's dead."

Her breadstick broke and flew across the table onto Mr. Forten's plate.

"Sorry."

"Sorry? You should be sorry! We're paying out left and right, and I want to know why. The probability is all off. Are you approving people you know are sick?"

"That doesn't even make sense." She looked at her face in the knife blade. For a second, she could see Mrs. Lister in the hospital. "Look, boss, you checked the paperwork, right? You know there was no pre-existing on any of them."

Mr. Forten signalled the waitress for another drink. He also pointed her own breadstick at her.

"I'm just saying that it looks bad. It looks bad, *and* the numbers are pulling us down. This is a business, Suzanne, one I've worked hard to build and one I thought you understood. You know, it isn't just anyone I take under my wing."

He reached across and laid a hand atop hers. His palm was clammy.

Suzanne carefully extricated her hand from his and nodded.

"And I've been grateful for your help."

Until the Grahams.

After potatoes gratin and beef bourguignon, she arrived home. He had wanted to drive her, naturally, but Suzanne hurried off to the bus. She put her feet up on the sofa and turned on the late news. Terrorism and scandal. How much longer would she be able to hold her job?

She was in the park reading Tennyson, wondering how the splendour actually fell on castle walls, but knowing it did, when she saw him. He looked young— buzz cut, a pair of baggy pants. She felt long past this, or any other, kind of youth.

There was a gracefulness about him that she supposed could be attributed to his skills as a skateboarder, but he carried no skateboard. He was practicing something, sliding himself along the surface of the earth. At one point he smiled to no one but himself. He performed intricate hand manipulations that flowed so smoothly that they left her mesmerized.

Tai chi?

It didn't look like tai chi. She had seen people in the park in rows. She'd also passed the tai chi club on her way home and seen the students in the picture window.

This was something else. It was almost as if he was dancing with an invisible partner.

Blow, bugle, blow!

It was all well and good for Tennyson to set the wild echoes doing whatever they wanted to. How long since she had thought of castle walls? Since she had walked through afternoons with music in her head.

Sweep. He turned his body.

Around on his heel.

He turned again.

Tennyson almost making her believe that her echo

was capable of moving from soul to soul. That her echo would grow forever and forever.

Had she lost this much? This ease of movement? She saw herself, a woman alone in a park on a Saturday afternoon, nineteenth century poetry in hand, a person who, except for a lifetime of abnormal visions, was slipping into the pit.

Tuesdays—lunch at the Chinese place.

Fridays—over for Italian.

Every second Thursday—clothing to cleaners.

She closed the book and headed down the dirt path. She was twenty-eight going on fifty. No wonder Mr. Forten was putting the make on her.

When she got home, she looked around her small apartment. There were not enough windows. Her hoya plant was sick. Three weeks' worth of weekend papers were piled by the door, foundation of a fire hazard.

Fire Engine Sue.

She was going on thirty.

This put the "c" in crap.

•

She spent the night walking, stopping on the bridge. She'd forgotten, she'd actually forgotten, that there was a river in the city. The bridge was usually an elevated traffic jam, but at night it was quiet. She could not feel anything here, though surely there were echoes of those who had stood here before she had. Whether they jumped or fell or were pushed, they were gone now, like Carla, and she felt no vibrations from their shaking hands, sweating in the cool air.

When she was a child, she had wondered about her opposite, the bearer of glad tidings. How different her life must have been, doling out hope and sweet news and never, never standing on a bridge in the middle of the night.

Of course, a woman on a bridge at a late hour almost guaranteed a response. She could see the police car out of the corner of her eye, but she continued staring down at the dark water. It was so different from the little river, stream really, where she'd grown up.

"Excuse me, ma'am..."

Ma'am.

The officer was calm and moved very slowly, his hand out in supplication.

She looked at him. He was about the same height as Annie.

"Are you okay?"

She wasn't sure what he meant, so she said nothing.

"Uh...we're just out patrolling, and we saw you...you know, all by yourself here on the bridge, and we just want to make sure everything's okay. You been here long?"

Here at the edge. Yes, she'd been here for a while.

The officer was right beside her now.

"See? Things are okay. Things are going to be okay."

Of course things were going to be okay.

"Let's go and sit in the car for a while."

It was a good night for stars. She could make out the Dippers. She wasn't sure what was going on over in that corner of the sky, some stellar confusion. Maybe the stars hadn't decided what they wanted to be yet. The choices endless: the sea goat; the water-bearer; the twins, Castor and Pollux, Castor the horseman and Pollux the boxer. She wondered if there was room up there for other celestial beings. A boy on a dragon, his wild hair a gaseous mist around the brightest light, his head.

It was odd not having anyone to call. The police officer at the station actually looked sorry as she pressed for details.

Mr. Forten was not happy to be pulled out of bed. He arrived with a grumpy yet surprised look on his face. It took him some time to convince the officers that Suzanne was, in fact, a responsible employee who had been in at work only that day. There must have been some mistake.

"Why didn't you tell them who you were and what you were doing there?" he asked. "What were you doing there?"

Looking at the stars?

Alone, at two thirty in the morning.

The stars were luminous; they had momentarily baffled her.

"Baffled...."

"Baff....you bet I'm baffled! Look, do you need some time off work? Just say so, and I'll arrange something. This...this is unacceptable."

The stars had confused her.

"You're right," she said. "It is."

<u>1992</u>

No one had seen Suzanne in months. After the initial panic, a kind of numbness set in. She had given up her apartment, it would seem. Annie Fournier Robertson had been contacted by the landlord. Had the sister called in the cops?

The police had followed up on Annie's concerns,

especially when Suzanne's employer had confirmed her disappearance from her position at the insurance company.

Her parents were beside themselves. What were they supposed to do? They informed police of Suzanne's past emotional difficulties, refusing to use the word "mental." But she'd held her job for years! She hadn't, to anyone's knowledge, had an episode in recent memory.

"What if something's happened to her?" Adele Cardinal cried as her husband paced the floor.

Everyone thought it was strange that, once the police learned of her previous brushes with mental illness, their intense interest waned. They seemed to push their chins back in line with their bodies; their stances relaxed. After all, the streets were teeming with mental cases. They would keep an eye out, of course, but theirs were full-time jobs, as it were, and temporary citizens who slipped in and out of the city's consciousness were not a priority. Suzanne Cardinal would turn up.

Three months passed.

Annie didn't like talking about Suzanne to Ty, and who could blame her? His upscale sports accessories store was in trouble, and he was spending all his time in meetings and on the road. Zara was in Grade Three, a demanding little girl. And Robert and Adele were barely functioning, which everyone understood, given the circumstances. Robert was being more attentive to Adele, a backhanded blessing and something Suzanne would have found ironic if she were there.

But she wasn't there.

Misogi (Purification)

T his is what happened.
It was easier down by the river. Things had their
own integrity: ducks bobbed in and out of radial tires,
plinked their beaks against empty beer cans; and
frogs—oh, she could hear the frogs again!—peeped
and ribbited beneath the neon algae.

Arrowhead ferns swayed in the passing breeze,
reminding her of everything, of Jule moving on the
dance floor, Mrs. Reidel's laundry on the line. There
was a fishing line wound up in the weeds, on the end of
which was a shimmering yellow-green fly.

"That's a beaut. Catch something nice with that."

She jumped. Turning, she saw the boy from the
park, the one she had watched that day.

"'Course, I doubt you'd want to eat anything you
caught in this part of the river."

He smiled. His face was completely open. "Been here
long?"

She knew how it looked. How she looked...she had
forgotten herself awhile. The cracked fingernails, the
smeared hands. She felt like she had been here for
seasons and storms and solstices.

So he took her with him. There was a room, he said,

above his dojo. It was for visiting students, or a Sensei in town for a seminar. She could stay there, he was sure.

So she went with him.

The first two days she slept, waking only for brief periods and always with a leaden body she could barely lift off the sleeping mat. Her friend, Ewen, brought her steaming soups and dumplings from the Asian take-out nearby. She ate and slept.

On the third day, she stood up, walked shakily to the shower and stood under it until the water ran ice cold. The towels were thin, so she wrapped herself in several. She put the foul pile of garments she had peeled off at the edge of the room. She curled up in the towels and rested.

When Ewen returned, he threw the filthy clothes into a plastic bag and took them away. He came back with a pair of white cotton trousers and a T-shirt.

"Gi bottoms and a T-shirt. It's all that's around. It's what we wear." He added that there was a top that went with the cotton pants. "I'll find you one later. Don't worry. They're clean."

"Is this a church? Downstairs? Some kind of a church?"

He shook his head, his smile close to a laugh. "No. It's a dojo. It's where we practice Aikido."

Her brain turned over the word, but she had no picture.

"Uh…a martial art. A spiritual martial art."

Like karate? Kung-fu? David Carradine?

"I talked to my Sensei…my teacher. He says there's nobody coming in for a seminar for a while, so you can stay here."

She looked around the neat, tidy room. It *felt* like an upstairs room.

"Thank you…and him."

"Uh…when you're up to it, you know, strong enough, you might want to take your turn keeping the dojo clean. We take turns. You're not a student, so you might not clean the tatami, the mats, but you could help with the bathroom and shower area and the storage shelves."

So much movement. So many things to move, to get from here to there.

She said nothing.

"Good. Well, gotta go down now, to practice."

Ewen bowed to her in his spotless white uniform, noticed she was looking at it, and said, "My gi."

She looked at the clothes in her hands.

"Get dressed. You can come down and sit on the stairs and watch the practice if you like."

And he was gone.

Suzanne took off the towels one by one. When she was naked again, she forced herself to look down at her body. Concave stomach, her small, high breasts. How old was she? Her hands were veined, but no more so than the leaves that grew one summer then blew away. Rocks had veins like these, chock full of ore more valuable than her blood.

But not to me.

She went to the stairs, then, and watched the circular turns, the enterings, the pins and rolls. This was a dance a body understood intuitively, a breath, and enter, a breath, and turn. The woman in the stairwell, bare feet curved around the edge of the step.

Ewen paired with someone in black flowing pants so wide they were like a long skirt or culottes. Ewen

167

attacked, but his force was welcomed by the black-suited man, embraced, one arm ghosting the attacker's, a shadow dance around his back, an invisible turn, and Ewen rolled away.

How much time passed, she had no idea. The ash on the end of the stick of incense grew, the picture of a Japanese founder stared from the wall, unwavering.

•

How old was she?

Her father had a theory, he told Little Sue.

"You're as old as your last thought."

Which puzzled the girl. Her last thought had been about how old she was.

"I just got here."

"Compared to the stars, yes," he said, pointing out the sweep of Orion's belt.

The stars did look old. Yet they were bright. How come old people didn't shine like that? Mrs. Reidel, for instance. Although she did smile her special smile when she took the Oreo cookie bag down for Suzanne.

•

Her mother told her she was the big sister.

"You're older. You're grown-up now. You're Carla's big sister."

•

"I used to be a big sister," she told Ewen one evening as

they were sweeping the steps of the dojo.

"That's cool. It's a good organization. My cousin did that."

"No, I mean...."

And didn't know why she said it. She'd taken to saying whatever she was thinking, which was surely a way to get into trouble. Hadn't she learned that much?

"Oh..." he read her face.

He read my face.

"Yeah, well, I used to be a son. My old man just couldn't give up the booze and the gambling. Know what he used to say? 'At least it's not drugs and women.' I have to say, he made me laugh."

Ewen held the dustbin for her.

"He's gone?"

"Yeah. Everybody was so *right*. You know. They wouldn't forgive him. Even me, I waited. But then I started going to see him, and I was with him when he died."

"How do you mean 'right'?"

"You know. Noble. Holier-than-thou. Man, give me impure, fucked-up people any day. They're at least still in the game."

They opened the front and back doors of the dojo and let the breeze through. Sitting out on the stoop, Suzanne thought about Ewen and his father.

"Was it hard?"

He had come down the steps behind her and now sat beneath her on the lower step, looking up.

"Seeing him die? Yeah. But, you know, it was hard seeing him live, too. We settled in and got comfortable with the whole thing, and in the end it wasn't bad."

A siren sounded a few blocks away. A woman was

picking up bottles across the street. They watched an old man pull a wagon along the sidewalk.

"What else did you used to be?"

It was a long time ago, and suddenly she felt very old. When was the first time she had the feeling that her life wasn't completely her own, that something could come over her that would enrapture her? She told Ewen about what she could sometimes see. About Fire Engine Sue. "I've been on the outside my whole life."

A girl on an ancient green bicycle rode by in the dusk.

"Outside of what?"

He was off to meet his brother and sister, he said. They got together every couple of weeks for a meal.

"You're welcome to join us."

How strange that would look, this young man with a stick woman tagging along. She shook her head, uneasy at this sudden gesture, and spent the evening on the upstairs balcony, watching the street. The lights were nice, even when the exhaust fumes weren't.

"You're the centre," he'd said. "From where you are, all the stars move around you. Don't you feel it?"

She sat on the balcony with her foot on the railing.

"You don't like something? You gotta be the one who changes it. My old man said that…ironically, I guess."

"Gandhi said it too."

"Yeah. I guess a lot of dudes said it."

Gandhi. India. She had forgotten India and Kashmir. Mountains used to float before her eyes as she fell asleep.

She remembered watching an old movie with her father one night. *The Mask of Dimitrios*, one of her

170

dad's standards. And there was a point at the end when the Sidney Greenstreet character got captured, and Peter Lorre turned to him and said, "Now you won't get to go to the Indies."

And she sat up in her chair and blinked.

There were things you would not get to do. And it would hit you all of a sudden, the moment the universe of possibilities turned her black cape and walked away; that you would remain who and what you were forever. Unless, as Gandhi and the other dudes said, you made the change yourself.

She watched the young men and women repeating what they called *irimi tenkan*. Enter and turn. Enter and turn. *Tai sabaki*. How you move. Your floor exercises. Breathe. Breathe. *Kokyu*.

"Everything is *ki*," Ewen smiled, moving the jade plant closer to the window.

Energy, life force.

Suzanne caught herself smiling at the pair of flip-flops in the corner, one sandal kicked up, climbing the wall. Maybe old Cliffy was right, after all, when he talked to the water cooler.

And one day it was the most natural thing to step to the edge of the tatama, bow to O Sensei's picture and to the other participants, kneel back on her feet, in *seiza*, and begin.

•

Time passed. She now worked with Ewen and Anya and Dirk at the drop-in centre. Her clothes came from the donation bin. She was helping Angel with her spelling. Angel lived in a halfway house, "'cause I'm halfway to having a life," she said. Her system finally clear of drugs, she was trying to improve her basic skills so she might be in a position to get a job one day. She had, as she said, "given up whoring," and was surviving on her monthly assistance cheque.

Angel took a liking to Suzanne. She said it was good to deal with someone who had been there.

Suzanne smiled at her. *Been where?*

She worked with Angel, and with Murray, who couldn't read at all and who had injured himself ingesting lemon-scented cleanser, thinking it was a drink. And she took her turn making sandwiches for the lunch crowd, cracking and peeling dozens of hard-boiled eggs.

It was good, exhausting work, and at night she crept up the dojo stairs to the small room and slept soundly.

•

They were telling Beginning Stories one night, up on the roof. At first she didn't know what they meant. Ewen explained.

"Kind of like the mega-version of 'what did you used to be.' You know, the cosmic picture."

"Cosmic," Anya echoed, as she tended to do whenever Ewen was around.

They sat and crossed their legs. Suzanne could feel the gravel in her sandal.

"Okay, I'll start," Ewen stood up. Against the dark, rich sky he was darker still, the outline of a man with stars skimming his head.

"This is the story of the Sun Goddess, Amaterasu-O-

Mikami, known as the "Person Who Makes the Heavens Shine", one of the most important of all the *kami,* the Shinto gods. And it is the story of Susano-o-no-Mikoto, the Raging Storm, the Impetuous Male God, who is extremely powerful.

"Now, Susano is a bit reckless, and although he has a peaceful covenant with the Sun Goddess, he blows it by pissing her off. He breaks down the divisions in the rice fields, chokes up the irrigation ditches, opens the sluices—you know, things that will really anger the Goddess, who is there to make the rice grow. Oh…and he slathers excrement all over her sacred halls while she's in the fields for the harvest."

"What?" Anya explodes.

"Yeah. Impetuous. The Impetuous God."

"When I'm impetuous, I don't wear underwear," Anya informed everyone.

"So," Suzanne found herself asking, "what happened?"

A plane was in its final descent en route to the airport.

"Well…well, you don't want to piss off the Sun Goddess, you know?"

"It's not nice to fool Mother Nature," Suzanne murmured.

"What? Right. Anyway, she gets really angry, and she goes into her Heavenly Rock-Cave and closes the door. Darkness comes over all the earth. Like, really bad. No one can tell night from day. People can't see one another's faces."

Suzanne looked at the murky outlines of the people on the roof.

"So the Eighty Myriad of Gods have this meeting on

the 'Dry-Bank-of-the-Eight-Sand-Bank-River-in-Heaven.' They realize they'll have to make major appeasement. They make *nigite,* offerings of cloth, blue cloth made of hemp, and white cloth woven of mulberry paper. They make this mirror resembling the sun, out of copper brought from Mount Kagu. They weave robes. They string together five hundred jewels. Oh, and they build her this new sacred hall of the best timber and fill it with spears, shields and swords, and iron bells."

Suzanne could hear the bells when she sat very still.

"Lastly, they find a Sakaki tree, carry it to the Sun Goddess Amaterasu and lay the gifts on its branches. They speak of Amaterasu in glowing terms as the small bells tinkle. They offer prayers to her. I guess it works, because then Amaterasu, the Sun Goddess Who Makes the Heavens Shine, opens the Rock-Cave. They convince her to exit and head over to her new palace. When she does, the sun returns. The sky lights up once more and everyone is happy. And they cry, *'Ahare! Ahare!'* The sky is now alight. *'Ana omoshiroshi!'* How happy we are to see one another's faces. And they cry, *'Ana tanoshi!'* It is joy to dance with outstretched arms."

Ewen stopped speaking. He stood there on the roof, opened his arms and began to dance. Suzanne watched him until she felt tears running down her face. Everyone was getting up and swaying and turning.

Dancing.

A hand reached for her and she stood, gravel stuck to her pants, and she gazed up at a far star past the rooftop, lifted her arms and danced. *Misogi,* she thought. Purify.

Beginning Story

Daddy says we're double stars, and the house is the middle. We go around the house, Carla and me. Because there's two of us, and because of the house, we're pulled closer and we'll always be together. Even now that Carla's gone, Daddy says we're double stars in the sky, "bindery stars" he calls us.

This is the story of the teller of plagues, the voice of the drowning, the cries of the dying. Fire Engine Sue, Daughter of Doomsday, known to no kami. *Binary star, she and Carla, in elliptical orbit around the house, gravitationally bound, and singing songs.*

They are close in space, their colours yellow/yellow in the night sky. Astronomers measure their separation, call them double stars, add their names to those of Sirius and Procyon.

Never double. Never double, you fools. It is the fault of the lens on the hopelessly inadequate telescope. They are not true doubles, merely optical doubles, appearing side by side but in fact light years away. And the swiftly turning planet casts one off, leaving the other to hang in the firmament alone. The gravitational pull is broken, yet the Daughter of Doomsday clings to the fraying energy: lingering dust, a fondness for music, a lock of hair in a desk drawer somewhere.

Sorei Haishi (Ancestral Prayer)

1999

The rain comes down hard, but she walks lightly, imagining the spaces between raindrops, imagining the painted clouds on the ceiling of the Kamosu Shrine. There are serpent heads, bouquets, puffs of smoke. They float before her eyes and are perfectly at home on the ceiling, or in her eyes. The rain pools at the curb, and she submerges her toes in it. Wind rips the first red leaf from the maple tree and tumbles it end over end before her on the sidewalk.

The shrubs are patchy. Cedar is hard to grow well, especially when there are no green thumbs in the family.

She rings the bell.

This house, the trellis.

The door opens. Her father has aged. He is completely grey now, the lines at his jaw more pronounced.

"Suzanne…?"

It isn't really a question. It is a fishing line dropped tentatively into a stream.

"Hello."

"Hello…"

She has not expected his voice to break. The previous times she's seen him in the past few years, she's understood that his universe has done entirely well without the presence of her little planet. And now here he is, standing at the front door and sputtering.

"Oh my God…oh…"

Sputtering. The mole near his ear has grown.

"Dad…can I come in?"

He holds open the door and, in doing so, his arms, and as she passes into the house, she can hear him sigh painfully.

The living room is pale rose now. She puts down her bag and removes her shoes.

"You don't have to…"

The carpet is thicker than the mat she sleeps on. She warms her toes in its pile.

"Uhm…your mother's out at the moment. Should be back soon. Can I fix you something? Tea?"

He is making helpless movements with his hands. It reminds her of the way he used to hold them when he ran in the basement.

"Tea, Dad. That would be nice."

The word "Dad" comes easily to her lips. She can't believe how quickly it slides down from the brain. Like the other name.

"Mom out shopping?"

Her father leans in from the kitchen, the tea water boiling. "Sorry, just a minute."

She hears him pouring water and setting the pot down. Then he comes in to sit with her.

"Sorry."

"Mom. Where is she?"

He glances left and right, actually shifting back and forth like a B-movie actor, like when she was young and they were spies together.

"She's gone to see your sister."

"I haven't seen Annie. How is she? How is Zara?"

"She's...fine."

He's knotting his fingers.

"What? Is it Ty then? What's wrong with Ty?"

Her father's eyes. "We think he's hurting Annie."

Annie Fournier, who once picked up a boy in math class and tossed him out the door, who dumped a girl into a snow bank for calling Suzanne names?

But it makes some sense of the inexplicable vision, the real reason she's come back. Two figures on an embankment. Unclear, but one is larger. Suzanne had thought: a man and a woman. But a woman and a child? Her evening sweats over this picture, the sudden flashing brightness, air thick and encompassing. Choking, noise, noise, silence. That it should be Annie...that Suzanne should be the one with feet planted firmly?

Suzanne mechanically looks for mugs and spoons, pouring her father's tea as he trails her around, telling her the story of Annie and Ty Robertson.

"Your mother suspected it for some time," he says apologetically, as if he has had his own head so far wedged as to be useless.

"Your sister's been secretive. She cancels on us without notice, and one time when your mother persisted and showed up at the house, Annie answered the door with a bruised wrist and a welt on her face."

Suzanne can see Ty clearly, his truck-sized body leaning into Annie as they speak. She can see Ty holding the infant, Zara, in one hand, cradling her up his arm. They are big arms, the arms of Ty Robertson.

"You let Mom go there alone?"

"We both go," he says abruptly. "Have gone. We try to go when he's at some business thing. Your mother insisted on going today, because she was hoping to talk Annie into coming back with her."

"But…"

"I had a doctor's appointment."

Defensive. The same old checks and balances.

They drink their tea. It must suddenly occur to her father that he has not asked her one thing about herself because he says, "You scared your mother as well."

Welcome home.

When Adele Cardinal arrives, she hangs up her jacket, turns, and sees Suzanne. Suzanne immediately regrets the timing, as her mother has obviously been through a lot today. It is on her face.

"Sue…Suzanne," her mother manages to get out before collapsing into the nearest chair.

"Hi…uh…I should have called."

Suzanne moves the footstool over for her mother, but the woman continues staring at her.

"I can't believe it's you. Where have you been?"

"Well…you know, eh?"

Her mother's eyes accuse, yet betray as well a sadness that goes far beyond anger. Suzanne looks for and finds the bottle of brandy, always her father's last resort, and pours her mother a generous drink.

"I'm all right!" her mother snaps.

Adele, as well, has aged. She has kept her hair dark, but the crows-feet define her eyes, and her whole expression has sagged. Suzanne sees some of herself in that face.

"Dad told me."

"Told you...what...Robert!"

Robert has been summoned and enters with a firmly etched expression of guilt on his face.

"You told her...I didn't want..."

They didn't want outsiders in on this sordid bit of the story.

"Mom..." Her mother pinned by the word. "She's my sister. Of course I want to know."

And there, amid the brandy snifters and the tea mugs, in the rose-coloured living room, they all arrive at the same place, at the same time.

"She's my sister," Suzanne repeats, to her mother's astonishment.

Everything spills, tears, stories of Annie and Zara sitting in the mall until it closes; Zara's tantrums; Annie's quiet pills and drinks.

"I told her, today, to come home," Adele said, swivelling her body toward Robert in solidarity.

"We...we want her to come home."

"Oh, and you, too..." her father's disappearing voice. Suzanne and Carla in their sundresses, ice cream cones askew.

Suzanne smiles. "Don't worry about me. But, I agree, Annie and Zara have to get out of there."

By the end of the evening, much has been discussed about Annie and how to deal with the situation. Very little has been said about Suzanne's return. She has probably just shown up for the moment and will be off again anytime. Or she's found a new way to break their hearts. She can't be counted on for anything.

Oh, but I can.

Not binary, after all, but persistent yellow in the night sky. Not a star to wish on, but a star to count, leaning back in the damp, webby grass, ears and eyes awake.

When Ty Robertson is in town, he goes into his office around nine thirty a.m. Suzanne sits with her back to the neighbour's oak tree and peers at the house. Sure enough, at 9:38 a.m., the front door of the ranch-style house opens, and Ty Robertson pushes out. His large chest and arms bulge in the pale cream golf shirt, one of this year's casual line, no doubt. He does not look back or wave, he just squeezes into his Mazda Miata and backs out of the driveway.

That was easy.

Suzanne waits until the car turns the corner, then she dives out from behind the tree and walks briskly up the path to the door.

No answer. She has been watching the house since dawn, and she knows Annie is in there. She pounds louder on the shiny brass knocker.

Shuffling behind the door, then...

Oh. Annie Fournier. Red eyes in a face that hasn't looked that wan since she arrived at the Cardinal house all those years ago.

"So," Annie says, "what took you so long?"

Almost a hint of the old voice.

Suzanne follows her into the front room.

"Where've you been?" she asks. "You want a drink?"

It is not yet ten in the morning.

"It's Happy Hour," Annie responds to the unspoken observation. "It's always Happy Hour."

She pours herself a scotch and swirls it in the glass, turns and points at Suzanne with her drink hand.

"Here are my questions: ONE—Did they send you? TWO—Why did you come? THREE—Where have you been?"

"No. I wanted to. And around," Suzanne says.

Flicker of a smile?

"Trained you well," Annie mutters into the glass. "So...you here for a social visit? You look strange."

"Thanks."

"No. It's not bad, really. Kind of *Sound of Music* meets ninja. You do poverty well." She shakes her head at her own comment and casts a glance, then a wave, around the room. "As you can see, I've got it made."

Suzanne stares. This is Annie. Sarcastic. Pointed. This is Annie Fournier. So how can the other be true?

"I heard something." A pause that crouches between them. "About you. About Ty."

"Oh, yeah?" That's a new tone. Angry, but not angry enough.

"Yeah. Rumour is Ty's been hitting you."

She stiffens. "Says who?"

"What do you mean 'says who?' Who cares! Besides, you know they're worried about you. And what about Zara?"

Annie Fournier turns. "You ought to know not to believe rumours, Suzie Q. Remember the ones about you? You got to play nutso because somebody started a rumour. You lost part of your fucking life because of it!"

"And you?" Suzanne enters. *Irimi.* "What are you losing, Annie?"

Her sister's broad shoulders droop, then begin to shake. She does not look up at Suzanne.

"Shit." Suzanne draws herself around Annie, the smell of scotch in her nostrils.

It turns out Ty has been having some business problems and is under a lot of pressure. It turns out that Annie is more annoying than anyone would have guessed, and the daughter is an absolute terror to live with. It turns out that if it weren't for Annie, Ty would be a complete success, as he was before he hooked up with her.

"You mean, married?"

That same comment had earned Annie a swipe across the face.

"I don't get it," Suzanne keeps saying, still small beside the formidable Annie Fournier.

But Annie can shrink, which Suzanne has never realized. Annie does something with her eyes and is suddenly less than she was. Look at her now. An expression Suzanne hasn't seen before, her shoulders hunched. Smaller. Smaller.

"Come back with me. We can pick Zara up from school."

"Oh, yeah, she'd love that. Her weird Auntie Sue with the front-and-backless shoes. "

"They're just sandals. They're made somewhere in eastern Europe."

"They look insane."

"Come with me."

She cannot tell Annie what she has seen, the two figures on the edge. She cannot assume things about this bond. It is enough that Robert and Adele Cardinal are worried, that Annie shakes and that Suzanne is here.

"I can't leave."

"Why not?"

"I…just can't. Get off my back."

"All right. Okay. You won't come back with me. Well, I'm staying here."

"What do you mean? You can't…"

"Set up the cot, Annie, and pass out the plushy towels, 'cause I'm moving in!"

Annie is going to cry. "You can't stay *here!*"

"Oh, I've stayed in worse. I'm here, Annie. Get used to it."

"It isn't me. He'll be…oh, you have to leave," she pleads.

"Then, throw me out."

Here is a scene from a long-ago movie. Annie Fournier versus the wispy presence of Suzanne Cardinal. But Annie's powers have flown. She stands but cannot stand steady.

They both sit on the front steps, waiting for the school bus. Birds pick ridiculous patterns over a spot of lawn that is being seeded. Annie has put out a bowl of cherries and is distractedly throwing pits in the direction of the birds.

Zara is nine now, a Grade Four student at the public school in Annie's suburb. She is enjoying school, Annie says, although she is in trouble a lot. Her teachers say the girl seems to have difficulty focussing, and she has trouble controlling her temper.

"She got suspended once for pushing a kid into a toilet cubicle and holding her hostage there."

Lovely. Except for the hostage part, Zara could be a

miniature Annie Fournier.

"She gets these screaming fits sometimes. I'm just warning you," she says.

The school bus stops three doors away, and soon the reddish-blonde head of Zara Robertson emerges from the bus. She turns in her driveway and stops short. A cat scoots across her path.

Annie waves her up, but Suzanne notices the reluctance in the child's step, feels it in her own feet.

"You remember your Auntie Sue? You haven't seen her in a long time."

The girl looks anything but shy, but there is that hesitancy again, the jitter in the arm and the rapid blinking of the eyes.

"Hi," Suzanne says. "You're getting tall."

The girl looks for an opening between the two women and rushes through it, her knapsack hitting Suzanne as she barrels past.

"Don't eat crap!" Annie yells after her. "Busy. She goes swimming. There's soccer. Today's swimming but we'll skip it. She hates it," Annie adds before Suzanne can protest.

Suzanne says. "I practice martial arts."

"You? You kill me."

After several hours with Annie, Suzanne begins to feel more comfortable. The same cannot be said about Zara, who sits in her room reading or playing on her computer.

"Come set the table for dinner," Annie calls to the closed door.

Annie's words fall on deaf ears, so Suzanne finds the plates and cutlery.

"I tried calling him at the office."

"To warn him," Suzanne finishes.

"He wasn't there."

Suzanne can tell that Annie is bothered. But there's nothing for it. Suzanne sits in the living room and flips through a large coffee-table book about water.

"Water," Suzanne says.

"Nice photos," Annie says and they both chuckle. It is precisely at this moment that Ty Robertson walks through the door. Perspiration stains the underarms of his shirt. He stops dead in his tracks when he sees Suzanne.

"Hello," she says. A clean *irimi*.

Annie is on her feet. "She's come by. She's visiting. I tried calling you. Isn't that great? Suzanne being here?"

He doesn't glare. Quite the opposite. His face takes on a studied expression. "Ah, yes, Suzanne."

He goes over to pour himself a drink. "Can I get you ladies anything?"

Annie looks back at Suzanne.

"Uh…sure," Suzanne says. "Whatever you're having."

"Me too, babe," Annie Fournier calls.

Suzanne watches Ty at the credenza. His back is to her; she can see the tight muscles in his neck working. But he turns with a smile on his face.

"Here we go. Martinis all around."

They each take a glass.

"Well," Ty looks at his wife, "aren't you going to toast?"

Annie glances at Suzanne. "To company," she says lamely, and gulps the drink down.

"Don't be a pig, honey," Ty says.

Suzanne meets his expression mid-air. "Zara's tall. Lanky. Two tall parents."

Ty remembers Zara. "Where is she? *Zara!*" From the bedroom down the hall a voice replies. "Don't what me! I'm home, goddammit!" He turns to Suzanne. "Kids," he explains. "Get in here!"

A door creaks, and Suzanne hears slow footsteps on the hardwood floor.

"What?" the girl says from the living room archway.

"Can't you see we have guests?"

Zara steps in, just. "I know."

"Did you do all your homework?" Annie asks.

"Not all of it. I'm stuck on the story."

"Well, your Auntie Sue is good at English. You should hear the stories she used to tell," Annie says.

"Really?" A look, almost curiosity.

"Maybe she'll go help you while I finish making dinner."

Annie nods hopefully in Suzanne's direction.

"Uh…sure."

Suzanne doesn't want to leave Annie alone with Ty, but she gets up and follows Zara.

It's a kidroom, walls of stuffed animals.

"I'm not allowed to play with those."

Puzzles, boxes piled like blocks, one atop the other.

"So, Zara, what's your Lit question?"

The bed is very neatly made, for a nine-year-old's effort.

"It's about *The Secret of Nimh.*"

"Oh, sorry. I don't know that book. I've heard the name. What's it about?"

"You know. Secrets. Magic. Mice."

"Listen, Zara, suppose you tell me a story of your own."

The girl is careful, so careful as she rounds the territory, settling at last next to Suzanne on the floor.

They lean their heads back against the bed.

Half an hour later, dinner is served. Zara's story was interesting in the way that it killed off most of the adults and left the children eating red licorice and Cocoa Puffs.

Very brittle, this meal. Ty says nothing, sitting posture-perfect in his captain's chair. Annie Fournier passes everything around the table twice and apologizes for the carrots.

"It's okay. I hate carrots," Zara offers.

They finish up the dishes. There is no small talk. What can they chat about? Suzanne's disappearance from her job and her life? Zara's temper tantrums? Annie's unexplained bruises?

After, Suzanne and Annie do dishes.

"He's trying with Zara, you know."

"He's trying with everyone. Sorry." She hands tall Annie the platter to put up on the top shelf. "Does he know I'm staying?"

Annie catches her finger in the cutlery drawer. "Damn! No. See? I'm a klutz."

Annie finds Zara in the garden. It's a lovely garden—how does Annie find the time?

"Do you help your mom with the garden?"

"You mean Dad. He likes to come out here and 'muck around.' That's what he says. He makes me do the weeding."

"Your Dad made this?"

"He planted all these."

"Nice. They're really nice."

Lilies and blue flowers she doesn't know. Lots of colourful ground cover.

"Everything's perfect," Zara says.

They talk about *The Secret of Nimh* in the garden. It's about bravery, Zara thinks.

"Are you brave, Zara?"

The girl looks up, but not directly at, Suzanne. "No."

"Is your Mom brave?"

Zara rejects a flower she has picked, hiding it in among the leaves. "My Mom's fine. I like her just like she is."

Yelling from the house.

"Oh, by the way, Zara, I'm staying to visit for a while."

Can she tell Annie about the vision? It is indistinct—she can't make out the figures, yet she feels she needs to be here.

There's nothing to tell.

Ty is gone in the morning. Breakfast is quiet. Annie has an appointment at the salon.

"Why don't you come along? My treat: massage, manicure, pedicure, facial, the works."

Suzanne glances down at her toes, the chipped nails, the rough heels.

"No. I'll stay here, if that's okay."

It is not only okay, but Suzanne's promise to pick Zara up at the park after soccer gives Annie a whole day to herself, and she gives Suzanne a thumbs-up.

"I'll get my hair coloured, too."

"You do that?"

Annie Fournier? A massage she could understand, after the years of sports. But the works? As if in answer, Annie says, "Ty likes me buffed and polished."

Suzanne pushes down the strange acid creeping up

her esophagus. "You look okay right now, you know."

She can tell that Annie can't hear her.

Three nights later, Zara has a nightmare. She wakes up screaming, and Suzanne rushes in from the guest bed in the den. Suzanne knows nightmares. The child is sweating and muttering incoherently.

Annie is right beside Suzanne.

"She does this sometimes," Annie says.

They sit the child up, and Annie speaks to her in a measured voice, rocking her softly. She strokes Zara's damp hair and uses the top sheet to wipe her beaded brow.

"There you go now," she says over and over. Suzanne stands back. This Annie. A mother anyone could be. She looks at her sister in awe.

Suzanne returns to the den only to find the La-Z-Boy occupied. Ty, in his underwear, is stretched out in it. He fixes his eyes on Suzanne.

"She's okay, I think. She's quieted...Annie...uh... Anne's with her."

He lifts one leg over the arm of the chair so that his bulging crotch faces her. Suzanne is about to look away, then she squares her stance and is in good *hanmi*, ready.

"Why aren't you somewhere else?" he asks slowly in a soft voice that should be reserved for more intimate moments.

"What?"

"Why aren't you wandering in ditches, or in an asylum somewhere?"

"They were full. So I'm here."

"Here might be a bad idea." His voice, his crotch, become aggressive. "This is a mistake, you know.

You've got the wrong end of the stick," Ty says.

She would welcome a wooden stick right now, a *jo* she could use to send this man flying. "Hey, I'm the crazy one, remember? You can't fool me."

A noise that is almost a growl emerges from his throat. "Leave us alone."

Suzanne smiles but says nothing.

"You hear me?" He almost rises from the chair but sinks back.

"A well-named chair," Suzanne mutters. She nods to him as she backs out of the room.

"I'll stay in here with her tonight," Suzanne tells Annie. "I have a lot of experience with nightmares."

The floor is comfortable, the area rug cozy. Zara's breathing is even and regular. Toys vie for space, but the spot on the carpet is empty except for Suzanne.

"He didn't come back to bed. He slept in the den," Annie says.

"Yeah. Well I guess Zara woke him up, and he went in to watch TV."

"You shouldn't have slept on the floor."

"I always sleep on the floor."

"Yeah?"

"Yeah. Look, Annie. I can't protect you. Physically, I mean. I can only help you protect yourself. Please come with me."

"Will you stop? You show up, I haven't seen you in ages—because you took off! How cool is that? And you come here judging me, judging my life. At least I *have* a life. I have a husband. A kid. Look at you. No, no, look at you! What gives you the balls to criticize anybody?"

Her eyes are so tired. It takes a lot out of her to deliver this speech. Suzanne nods.

"I know. I know, Annie."

Zara is now her buddy. She hugs Suzanne and clings more than she needs to. Auntie Sue is okay with it. After all, she's strange, too. She knows about bad dreams, and yelling, and people who disappoint.

Ty doesn't come home for dinner. The captain's chair is empty, but nobody else tries to sit in it. In the evening, they watch TV. Zara likes light comedy; Annie likes sports.

"What about you, Auntie Sue?

"Any travel shows on?"

"Bor-ing!" Zara sings.

"I didn't know you had mats down here!" Suzanne exclaims the following day, which is a Saturday. Annie and Ty sleep in on Saturdays, so Suzanne and Zara have the run of the house. The entire basement floor is covered in gym mats.

"They were supposed to be for my sleepovers, but I don't have any."

Suzanne takes Zara's hand. "I know what to do with mats."

They practice in secret and in silence.

Fall, Zara. We will learn to take a fall.

Somersaults come naturally to Zara, and she has only to adjust her angle, to use her shoulder and arm, then she has the many forward and backward rolls, something that took Suzanne nine months to accomplish.

Ukemi.

"Show me more!"

Rei. Bow.

Ty wants her gone, and Suzanne is not sure how much more time she has, but Zara's hand fits well in hers, as her other hand plays with the fringe on Suzanne's scarf.

"Is it true my mom's not your real sister?"

"Who told you that? Your mother?"

"Nope. It's just that the kids at school say if someone's adopted, they're not your real family."

Suzanne holds Zara's hand between her own and gives it a shake. "You tell your friends they're wrong, okay? Your mom is my sister, and you're my niece."

"And my dad?"

"He…he's my brother-in-law."

The brother-in-law is circling. Is it only Suzanne who feels his eyes and his intent? She takes Zara out for the day. It is useless to buy her things. They go to the public library, a place she's never been. Zara is amazed that it has more books than she does.

"But I have more toys."

There is a storytime on, and though it is meant for little children, Zara sits on the carpeted stairs, fascinated by the middle-aged librarian who is reading her a story.

"You want to go and visit your grandparents?"

Zara isn't sure. Everything is strained through the lines on her father's forehead. She doesn't really know her grandparents, except for the haunted afternoon knocks on the door that have all but stopped.

"Come on. They'd like to see you."

Suzanne's father is mowing the front lawn when they walk up from the bus stop. A smile breaks across his face.

"I'll get your mother. Your grandmother."

He drops the manual mower and blazes into the house.

"They're okay, really." Suzanne squeezes Zara's shoulder.

Adele is at the front door with tears in her eyes.

"There you are," she keeps saying.

There you are. How good it is to see one another again. Beginning Stories.

Robert Cardinal nods at Suzanne as if she has done a good thing, the right thing at last.

"Where's Annie?"

"At home. I just took Zara out for the day."

Over biscuits and pop, Zara shyly talks to her grandmother in the kitchen. Robert points Suzanne to the back porch. Once outside, he says, "You can't take her back there."

"Dad, what can I do? Annie's there. She's Zara's mother. And she won't leave."

"That child needs a calm place."

Calm? Images flash: Suzanne, the fights, the pacing, the names.

"I know."

"Is it as bad as we thought?"

The birds are feasting at the feeder. Dusty leaves hide reddening tomatoes.

"He's not a good man."

They decide to call Annie and ask whether Zara could stay overnight. When Annie answers, she says Ty is out. "But he'll be here for supper. You've got to get Zara back. He'll hit the roof if she isn't here, especially if it's you who took her. Hurry!" she hisses.

After supper, Zara wants to sit in the yard around the barbecue pit. She is wasting marshmallow after marshmallow. She is in no hurry to leave. By the time Suzanne tells her it's time to go, she is sitting with her grandfather, who is telling her a story.

"There's a little horse in the sky," he says.

"What?"

"Equuleus, the little horse. It's the second smallest constellation."

"Can I see it?"

"Yes, but it's very faint, and you can't see it from here. But that doesn't mean it isn't there."

Suzanne leans against the door frame, remembering rare stories on summer nights.

"It's brightest in early August."

"That's soon!"

"Pretty soon. Its main star is called Kitalpha. I think that means 'part of a horse.'"

"Why is it a horse?"

"It's just what people thought. Some people thought the horse was given to the Gemini twins, the double stars, by Hera, the goddess. Other people think it was given to the twins by Hermes."

"I don't know any twins, or any gods."

The girl squeezes closer to her grandfather.

Suzanne makes her way back to the neighbourhood of long driveways and manicured hedges. Topiary looms in the early dusk. She moves quickly, running on the balls of her feet, keeping low. She looks like the thief that she is.

She opens the door with the key Annie has secretly given her. Quick check of the living room and den. She moves down the hall to the master bedroom. Annie is sitting on the bed, wrapped in a coverlet. Light from the bedside lamp glints off her sunglasses.

No sign of Ty. "Hey."

"You didn't bring her."

Suzanne removes Annie's orangey-pink glasses. "I didn't."

"Thanks. I mean it. She didn't need to see it."

Ugly, dark pink welt beginning. Suzanne sits beside her. "Neither do you."

"Yeah, well, he's pretty mad."

"Where is he?"

"I don't know. He stormed off."

"He...wouldn't be going to get her, would he?"

Ty bursting in on her parents...

"No...he's not done here yet. Look, go, will you? I don't want to make him even madder."

"You can't stay here, Annie!"

"Oh, but she can." *Tenkan,* and on the turn take in the towering shape of Ty Robertson, arms spread across the doorframe.

"Oh, Ty, leave her alone. She's my pathetic sister. Look, she's finally agreed to leave. Isn't that great? She's just leaving now, okay?"

Suzanne looks back at Annie, who pleads with her eyes.

Ty breathes, and his chest expands. This is what fuels him. Annie takes her arm, but Suzanne shrugs it off.

"You aren't fooling anyone," she tells Ty.

"What? What the fuck's that? The fuck do you mean by that?"

"Nothing, Ty, look at her. She's nuts, like you always said. You were right, see?"

"You don't fool me, Ty."

He glares.

"Annie and I are leaving. We're leaving now. Get out of the way, please."

Get out of the way. *Ikkyo.* Ewen's first exercise.

"Nobody goes anywhere until I say so. Sit down and shut up!"

It is better to stand.

"Come over and sit," Annie begs.

"Annie, I can't deal with both of you. And Ty," she says, knees ready, stance open, "it would be really good if you stopped this. We'll go, and we'll come tomorrow to talk things out, okay?"

The arrogance of it hits his brain. He advances quickly. *De ai.* Suzanne meets him on the upward arm of the strike, ghosts his movement, guides him forward, grabs his wrist and turns it. Ty follows his hand and topples.

Suzanne stares at the confusion in his eyes. "Please stop," she says.

His face, red and raging, bobs at her.

He is fast, but Suzanne's small body is faster.

"Get out, Annie! Go!"

Annie is riveted.

Ty is huge, but Suzanne can dance, she dances around him, turning beside and behind, and turning to face him again. *Tenkan. Double tenkan.* Physical shorthand. He is tiring, but she is not. Ty huffs and lunges; Suzanne enters. *Kokyu.* Breath Throw.

Yonkyu. Yokomen uchi.

Annie is standing now. "Sue...Sue...no!"

Suzanne is just coming around when he pushes her back to the floor, puts his hands around her throat and pins her.

"Nasty little piece of work you are," he mutters.

"They should have drowned you at birth."

It is a hold she can do nothing about, though she raises her legs and tries to grab his head with her feet. It distracts him, but she is the bug he is about to kill. Her head swims. She sees nothing, no flashes. No vision.

"No!" Annie, standing. "No, Ty!"

She hoists the lamp and brings it down on Ty's head.

Before he can even react, Suzanne has him in a hold, turns and pins him, and he is held face-down on the floor.

"Call the police," Suzanne says. "Now."

Annie stands with the remnants of the lamp.

"Annie. Put that down and call the police."

They will photograph the bruises on her neck, and on Annie's face. In the cruiser that follows the car with Ty, Annie takes hold of her hand.

•

They are eating cornflakes.

"I don't like cornflakes as much as Cap'n Crunch, but they're not bad," Zara says.

No one comments on Annie's sunglasses or Suzanne's eccentric ascot.

The radio says it's a good morning, except for the UV index, which is all one can hope for these days.

•

"Guys? I got to be getting back."

"Back where?"

Suzanne stuffs her kerchief in her backpack. "Work. I work at a shelter."

199

"Oh, Suzanne, you…" Her mother stops, surprised at her self-restraint. "You'll visit more often, won't you?"

"Yeah. Sure I will. Zara and I are doing a few things, so I'll be around."

Her parents hug her, her mother whispering her thank-yous, her father's touch on her shoulder lingering.

·

The air comes, cool and crisp, through her small window.

The figures on the edge. Annie and Zara? Ty and Annie? Annie and Suzanne? Suzanne lies on her sleeping mat, looking out the window at the stars. Equuleus, little horse. Gift to Castor and Pollux. And now to Zara.

The Planet Queen

2002

My father's cancer is now terminal. I say *now*, because I suppose there was a time when it was still a nub of uncertainty in his corporeal being, an inclination down a dark hallway. It has taken his lungs. He has not smoked in some time, but he breathes, now, as if his life depends on it.

I'm forty-two years old, and I've been thinking of the ones who were sloughed off the face of the earth, dead cells exfoliated so we could continue to shine. Soon it will be my father.

All the convictions, all the confusion. Now it's pretty simple. I see or I don't see. I say or I don't say. You can tell someone the outcome of a time-delayed televised game, but if they don't want to know, they don't want to know.

My father suspected something after I started coming around more often. He took out a brochure and shook it at me.

"My insurance company just sent me an estate planning guide. Can you believe it?"

"Of course I can. I worked in insurance, remember?"

The chemo has taken his hair, which was thinning anyway. No sleek waves under the fedora now. No shirts and ties either. My mother says she hardly recognizes him. Says she's glad he was never stocky to begin with, because the contrast would be too much.

•

"What is it today, Dad?"

Today he'll have some book ready. There's a chapter of this or a description of that. Mostly it's an excuse to listen to me drone on. It almost always puts him to sleep. The hospital bed is in the living room, and if I creep quietly enough, I can get out without waking him.

Annie hates being around the dying, but in a way that makes her the best of us all. She's strong enough to move Dad, and she makes him take his fortified shakes, no excuses.

We sit outside, Annie and me, watching Zara's dog, Brendan, dig in the yard. Zara's working at camp this summer.

"I can't believe he's fading," Annie says. And then she says, without a pause, "He took me in." Her voice is a deep pool. "I wasn't a bargain in those days either."

I look over at my sister. "You are now."

It was Annie who had cleared out my deserted apartment those years ago and paid the overdue rent when I disappeared. It was Annie who had packed away the dusty posters, the "beaded dingles," and returned my flowered cloth suitcase to me.

Never a word about it.

Annie raising the lamp over Ty's head.

203

Never a word.

.

It is a relief to get back home after a day sitting with Dad. I've offered my place to Mom and to Annie as a safe haven when they have to get away. But Annie takes a drive when she needs to blow off steam. And my mother will not leave him. I made her go get her hair done. Annie forced a restaurant lunch on her. But, basically, she will not leave him. She hurries back and putters in the kitchen or does the crossword beside him in the living room. One afternoon, she had just finished balling socks in the kitchen. She heard him murmur in the living room and promptly threw all the socks back in the basket, went in and re-folded them beside him.

Mysterious, their bond of stubbornness and loyalty.

Love, too, when you catch the details.

Something makes me want to find it. I spend twenty minutes rummaging in closets before I remember the storage unit, grab my flashlight and go down to the cellar. Unit seven, right opposite the empty one, in the dark corner. My high-school memory clicks in and the combination works. Three dollars and seventy-nine cents of security at the time. I still have nothing worth stealing.

I unearth the flowered bag, struck by the smallness of this suitcase that once held all I cared about.

Upstairs with a cup of chai tea, I open the bag, the zipper grunting and complaining.

Terrible drawing of Marc Bolan.

Dar's Birmingham concert poster, like something
from another century.
Right. It was another century.
My Book of Me, 1973.

They don't understand. I'm living my life now.
I'm on my way.

Notes about songs. Dar. Sewing projects. A mirror I
glued to the back of the second book.
The mirror, a sacred object. Mirror to catch the sun.
Sun Goddess in the Rock Cave coming forth,
illuminating the sky.
Ana omoshiroshi.
"How wonderful it is to see one another's faces again."

He lies down now, taking his breaths. He asks for
Saint Augustine, a prayer he knew as a boy, back when
he prayed. "Flood the Path with Light."
"Turn mine eyes to where the skies are full of
promise, tune mine ears to brave music…"

"I know a secret," I whisper into his ear. But fine
hairs filter out my voice, and he dozes on.
"Koto toishi iwane kine
Tachi kusa no kakiha o mo koto yamete."
"Moreover, silence was brought to the very foundation
of the majestic trees and to the standing grass,
Even casting silence down to each single leaf."

Silence, Dad. Just silence.
I hold his sleeping hand.

"What will I do now?"

She's keeping herself busy at the sink.

"You know, he never left. He could have," she wrings the end of the dishcloth, twisting all the old and painful stories.

"You could have left, too, Mom."

"What do I do now?"

She's small in my arms, my mother.

·

CARDINAL, Robert James. WW II Veteran, peacefully in hospital, July 15, 2002. Son of the late James Cardinal and the late Margaret Hammond. Survived by loving wife Adele (née Bonet) and daughters Suzanne and Anne (Fournier). Predeceased by daughter Carla. Dear grandfather of Zara. Resting at Roche and Magnusson Funeral Home. Funeral, July 20, 2002, St. Theresa's Church. Internment Villagegrove Cemetery.

The paper slips. This is it, then, the one-inch summary.

Bolan's "One Inch Rock". An early song about a boy shrunk down to an inch in height, but then a bopping beat starts, and his warbling voice, and no choice but to do the One Inch Rock.

Zara arrives in time for the funeral. She's sunburned and has a spider bite near her temple. She follows her grandmother around, helping with phone calls, ironing, buttons.

Annie and I sit out back.

"You think he was in a lot of pain?" she asks, not expecting an answer.

"He's okay now."

"She's going to be lost without him."

"She'll be okay."

"Oh. Right. Everyone's okay. Everybody's fine."

Annie's irritation with death and with me.

"Somewhere I read Katherine Hepburn saying that, after a certain age, the correct response to every question as to how you are feeling is 'fine.'"

"So?"

So.

To a Samurai, every day is a good day to die. It has to do with being prepared, with having lived one's life up until the very moment of death.

Ogen'ki desu ka? How are you?

Okagesema de. Fine.

The birds at the feeder; the hose spitting at the grass.

•

Been a long time since you've been in a church. Did they ever even go to this one? They never said. Maybe your mother…

Look at your mother. Zara has her by the elbow, towering over her. Annie looks uncomfortable in a very feminine navy dress. And you? Annie has forced you into a dark grey linen skirt. With the white blouse, you look even more the nun you've never been. Your hands are plain. All the years of nail polish, cheap rings, beaded bracelets. Now, a pair of middle-aged hands and you not knowing what to do with them.

They've asked you to speak. The priest will introduce you when it is time.

So the ancient ritual is enacted: the funeral prayers; water sprinkled; incense twisting smoky swirls around the casket on the bier.

·

Annie is crying now, and Zara moves to comfort her.

They are asking for you.

"Suzanne will now say something."

Everyone is waiting: even, it seems, your father. Candles gutter and bloom. Your flat shoes are silent as you waft up the aisle. You've never felt this lightweight; you're a few cells at most. Your mother's eyes watch you as they did when you were little, scoping out fears, love.

Okay. So you're here. And you do love.

The coffin is narrower than you thought it would be, and not as shiny as Mrs. Reidel's. Your eyes hate this so much; they close in protection, as does your throat. Your head spins, lawnmower wheels on the push mower your father is guiding over the grass. Look, he's unearthed your Annabelle's plastic hair bow, and it isn't even mangled! You wait until he's out of the way, then you run over and pick the pink bow up. How good is that? you ask.

He's over on the side, resting his elbows on the handle of the mower.

You going to help, here? I thought you were going to sing a grass-cutting song.

Only he can get you to stand slightly on your toes, open your scrawny throat and sing a song about cutting down green.

You look at the faces in the pews. "It's okay," you say.

Things get cut down all the time, green, tall, swaying, or stationary. It makes no sense that it should hurt. But we're here.

"It hurts because he was here with us. He was ours."

Your mother sobs. It starts a chain reaction. Annie, though, dabs her eyes in silence, much like the silence in which your own tears fall. You look to the casket, which tells you nothing.

"We'll miss him. He was ours."

And you look at the witnesses, safe in their heady, breathing selves.

What you don't say is: *we miss him, and we'll be joining him before we know it.*

And what you want to say is: *at least we're alive. We want so much to live.*

Zara says good things about her Grandpa. Annie, perhaps most touching of all, speaks, simply, of her early years. And of how things changed when she came to live with the Cardinals.

And, finally, it is over. Annie, Zara and Adele go in the same car. There is still the long drive to the country, to the town and the cemetery that holds everyone. You were supposed to travel in the same car as them. You would have, but for the couple at the back of the church. Funeral hangers-on? One never knew with whom Robert had dealings. You are reminded of Dickens, and Scrooge, and the "men of business" who would only attend his funeral if they were provided lunch.

I must be fed.

They will leave when the casket leaves.

But they don't. And when you turn to gather up your purse and jacket, they are suddenly right beside you.

The Hope Fiends.

Jule's eyes shining out from a face you almost recognize. Time has pulled her features down, but she is still thin and feral. Mark is softer, and his strange hair is almost completely gone.

"You..."

The Hope Fiends surround you, breathe on your neck, an arm across your head, forehead to forehead to forehead. A hand searches for yours, reclaims the space that holds your missing finger.

"We found you."

Mark has Lou Reed on the car stereo. "Walk on the Wild Side", which Jule thinks is inappropriate at the moment, which prompts a debate about Reed's influence on music, then a debate on the necessity of The Strokes' version of the song. Then silence.

"I'm just saying..."

You close your eyes and it is then, and the song is "Children of the Revolution", and they are arguing about whether or not the children of the revolution will be fooled. By what? By whom? And when you open your eyes, it is the highway and the backroads, and Jule and Mark.

You are swimming in them, your tears and grins and runny nose. Mark in front, eyes in the rearview. Jule beside you, holding on tight.

They came back. Who knew they would ever return? Mark and Jule. Past the train tracks where Charlie Donaldson tripped on gravity. The upstairs apartment over the store where Holly waited for little Falcon to be born.

"This...is my world," you whisper. Who knew they would ever visit your world?

And here.

Adele is propped between Annie and Zara. You are seized by a desire you hardly know and rip yourself from the car to join them. Your mother opens her stance, and her arms. You move with her, and enter.

You stand with them. Your friends stand by as well. Dar rests nearby, and Mrs. Reidel.

And your father enters the ground right beside Carla.

•

A city bar, the kind you've wasted time in, and the Hope Fiends across the table.

"We spent years away. Then we went back to school. Yeah, can you believe it? I got a social work degree, and Mark took a certificate in design."

"You've been together so long."

"Yeah. Don't remind us. We were going to have a family, you know, to spread the misery. But I guess all those years of self-abuse did its number. So it's just us."

Mark smiles, leans in secretively and says, "We were actually looking for you before we heard about your dad. " He is absentmindedly doodling on the table with his felt-tipped pen.

"Because of Bolan," Jule says.

Now it is you who smile.

"Don't you know? Haven't you been following it?"

"Following?"

And they tell you, you who do not know that twenty-five years have passed since Marc Bolan died.

What was Bolan's last hit?

A tree.

Twenty-five years.

And they tell you about the T.Rex Action Group and the plans to unveil a statue of Bolan at the Memorial Gardens right beside the tree he died in.

You realize you have always thought of it like this— the tree he died in.

"The bust is by a Québécois artist, Jean Robillard. You mean you don't know?"

"Man, I thought you'd be all over this," Mark says. "Guess you don't pay attention to the future any more, eh?"

Your head is clearing.

"Well," Jule grabs your hand, "we're going to London, to be there when they unveil it. Rolan will be there, and Mickey Finn."

Rolan Bolan, Marc's tiny son, a man now. And the other half of T.Rex, Mickey Finn.

"You'll come with us."

It's not really a question.

What is more foolish than this? You think. And then you think.

A block from the bar, you pass the Walterdale swimming pool, the letters on its sign always loose. Mark goes by and the sign now reads: "Walterdale Swim in   Poo."

•

Packing for a trip. It isn't India, and you aren't folding pashminas into airtight boxes. And it isn't Japan, and you aren't Amaterasu-O-Mikami, the Heaven Shining Great Goddess. But it is Jule and it is Mark. Arrange

your spindle tree, wear a scarf made of moss, hold
bamboo grass and leaves in one hand and a spear with
bells in the other, and dance at the sacred bonfire in
front of the heavenly Rock Cave.

Jule is at the door, her tired face medieval, her
child's body timeless. You gather her in your arms and
hold her close.

Ana omoshiroshi.

How wonderful it is to see one another's faces.

You hazard one final look around the place, your home.

•

When she was little, the flying she did was at the
amusement park. Her hair stood out straight when she
rode the Tilt a' Whirl, but she preferred when her father
spun her by the arms, in circles. That was long ago.

"So, did you know 9/11 was gonna happen?" Mark
asked.

The taxi driver's eyes jolted into the rear view mirror.

"No...I had flashes, but nothing definite.
Nothing...dramatic."

"Some gift."

Jule was studying people outside the window.

"We do the best we can with what we've got,"
Suzanne said, remembering her father's words, usually
spoken while sweeping up a broken plate or wiping
spilled coffee.

Jule burst forth with, "We're going to London!"

As though it had just occurred to her.

•

What did she know about England, after all? Bolan. Keats. The Beatles. The Queen. Queen. On the eternal shelf of human existence, The Queen of England perched next to Freddie Mercury.

England. Fog. Rain. Landscapes that dissolved in mist. Forensic travel.

Mark went over their itinerary once more. From Heathrow Airport, they would grab the Underground to Russell Square. Their hotel was nearby. On memorial day, they'd take the subway to Waterloo Station and get the bus from there to Bolan's Tree. It was Saturday, September 14, two days until the anniversary. Mark paid their taxi driver and went around to the trunk to help with the bags. Airport security was everywhere.

Sighing, Mark got into the check-in line, telling them it would take hours.

"Wander the Airportal," he ordered, so Jule and Suzanne walked around, stopping in the shops. Travel-sized toiletries, books, postcards, playing cards. The DutyFree. They bought coffees and sat in uncomfortable chairs that faced computer screens. Arrivals. Departures. Delays. Cancellations.

"Everybody has somewhere to go," Jule said, in a voice that might have sounded sad. Suzanne was glad to be there with Jule, but the years were the years.

They stared at the screens.

"Did it work?" Jule asked.

Suzanne swirled her cup. "What?"

"Your life. Do you think it worked out for the best?"

What a strange question. "Uh…yeah. It's okay. How about you?"

Jule smiled and shrugged. "I made a lot of mistakes."

"The Samurai say that a person who has not erred is dangerous."

"Hey, they'd know," Jule said. "Yeah, well, I would have liked a kid, I think. But it hasn't been too bad otherwise."

"We sound so convincing," Suzanne grinned.

"Two sure girls."

They went back to the line to relieve Mark, who immediately disappeared but not before promising to be back before they got to the counter. Jule put her headphones on and listened to Angelique Kidjo's African beat. Suzanne watched a little boy who was crawling out of his stroller while his parents argued. An elderly couple were sitting on their bags. Perhaps this is what it looked like when people died. They would sit on their luggage waiting for the end, then step onto the escalator and ride.

Mark returned with a rolled-up newspaper, which he was thumping in his hand. When he whacked it, his stomach jiggled a bit.

"Look!" he shrieked, shaking the paper in front of them.

"What, babe?"

"Look at this…this…."

"What?"

"Well…they did it already! They had the unveiling! It's over. Christ, they did it on Friday!"

Sure enough, the paper had run a photo of Bolan's adult son, Rolan, seated by the bronze bust of his father, underneath the tree. Rolan, skin black like his mother's, an intense and open face like his father's.

Suzanne read the article aloud as Mark groaned. The base of the bust was engraved. It said:

> *Sad to see*
> *Them mourning you*
> *When you are here*
> *Within the*
> *Flowers & the Trees*

Suzanne focussed, and Mark's complaining died away. She felt the thrill of Dar's voice, his hand grazing hers. You are here. An arrow on a map? A Shinto prayer? She watched Jule comfort Mark. How many centuries?
Okitsu kagami
Hetsu kagami.
Suzanne breathed.
Distant Mirror,
Close, Nearby Mirror.
Dar's hands chalky from the board, from the powder on the desks. Looking at her out of the corner of his eye.

Jule and Mark were discussing whether they still wanted to go. Jule was game, but Mark was disappointed.
"Why didn't they do it on the sixteenth?"
"Mark, maybe they couldn't," Suzanne said.
"I thought you cared about this!"
"I do. But we can still go. It will still be there. Really, it'll be all right."
"Oh yeah, great. Thanks for that."
Suzanne remembered a book she'd read in the university library one evening when she should have been working on her Byron essay. It was a book by a Chinese man who had been in London in the 1930s.

The book had caught her eye because of its unusual title. *The Silent Traveller in London*. Chiang Yee would wander around making notes about small, seemingly insignificant things, unable to communicate with anyone else. What he couldn't describe, he painted. He called them "odds and ends of observations" and had debated calling the book "A Chop Suey of London", because chop suey, or Tsa Tsui, meant a "mix-up of fragments." It felt like a Tsa Tsui of emotions, boarding the plane with Jule and Mark.

The Hope Fiends were in no mood to discuss serendipity and fell asleep with their heads touching. Suzanne had the window seat and felt the clouds slip beneath the wing. The sky would be very dark soon. Jule and Mark looked like they did as kids back on the branch of the tree behind the residence—defiant children, a little bit lost, but balancing in their sleep. Her head once fit in there, with theirs.

Her father had said something to her one afternoon. He'd been wondering whether a person was ever sure that he was ready to die, whether he'd done enough, learned enough.

He had no regrets, he said.

"Nothing you'd change?" she'd asked.

She saw it in his eyes, then. Change? Carla swam there. But regrets? No.

"I did the best I could," he said, and added, "That has to be enough to get you a night's sleep."

The hours swept over the plane. Suzanne took out her notebook, a far cry from the secret cloth books she used to hide. The sleek vinyl cover whistled at her as she slid it across the fold-down table. She pulled out her pen.

It is arrogant to write about what I know. Arrogant or hopeless. But there is this urge that makes us want to share our bits of days. Like Chiang Yee, painting an abundance of deer in Richmond Park. Why were there so many airy, dreamlike deer in Richmond Park that day? A farmer in the cornfield, looking up by chance to see the sky cracked open by a lightning bolt, looks left and right for a witness and knows at once that he is the only one who will take the imprint with him, a Shroud of Turin, a tattoo from summer camp, indelible and impressive and impossible to explain. But he will talk of it, over goats' milk and hard black bread. He will tell it and tell it, and it will remain bright in his eyes as the years deliver other skies.

Here. Here is my treasure, he will say.

And someone else, in a country rimmed with ice, will look down into a frozen pond and see a perfect leaf embedded, a fly in amber, a name pencilled in a book.

Here. Feeding birds in the park, a feathered beating life in my palm.

Here. My hand to the sky.

All we know is how much we love it. Here.

"Coffee? Tea? Juice?"

The attendant offered refreshments. The smell of coffee woke Mark, who put a finger up in reply. Suzanne noticed that he had doodled on the emergency procedures brochure, which now read "EMERGE" and "EXIT."

•

London. Heathrow was not London.

Heathrow was its own planet, endless day, endless bustle. Endless waiting again. It was well over an hour in line before they reached Passport Control.

Mark was diving into the fray now, looking for the bags. Jule looked a little shaky.

"We're here," she said, and Suzanne nodded.

London. Fast-moving. Suzanne couldn't imagine Dickens here, or any of his brood. Or Anne Boleyn walking past the Temple Bar and the Tower on her way to her coronation. Turning around and walking almost the same path in reverse, to her doom. All the monarchs and their minions, all the scaffolds and the blocks.

Roller blades now.

Mark taking pictures for a design project back home. Where was home?

She hoped Annie would take their mother up on the trip offer. Zara wouldn't mind staying with friends, and Annie and Adele had never seen the Rockies. Suzanne could picture the two of them standing on the ridge at the top of the Plain of Six Glaciers. But it would be the two of them, exactly, and not the figures in her vision.

"The Underground," Jule said, looking at her tourist book. "Funny they call it that."

"Why not? It's underground." The Velvet Underground. Lou Reed?

No. The Underworld. She was thinking of Bolan. *Dandy in the Underworld.* When did that come out? Just before he died.

"They also call it the Tube," Mark offered.

"I'm not getting into anything called the Tube," Jule said.

Mark had been studying the map of the Underground system.

"Look at their motto! 'Making London Simple.' Me, I think it's the Boddingtons."

They got on the Piccadilly line at Heathrow and shoved their bags into the storage space provided. Jule was quietly chanting the names of the stations from the map.

"Hounslow West," she murmured, as the train surfaced to cross a river. "Halton Cross," as the train dove again.

It was mesmerizing. Suzanne smelled cigarettes on clothing, a perfume scent that she hadn't smelled in decades. Charlie?

Curry.

"Where do we get off?" Jule asked again as the train pulled out of Ravenscourt Park.

"Well, no point in hurrying to the memorial site now. We should check in and dump our bags."

"At?"

"Russell Square."

The train pulled to the surface somewhere near Hammersmith, skimmed the earth at Baron's Court and dove again after that. In and out of the ground, aerating the planet.

Worthworms, the word came back to Suzanne.

"We're already at Leicester Square," Jule said.

"Remember me."

"What?"

Suzanne was swaying with the motion of the car. "Nothing. Nothing, an old song my dad knew. Remember me to Leicester Square? In Leicester Square? At Leicester…"

"Making London Simple."

They continued on to Russell Square and hefted their bags to the elevator. There was a lineup. One of the elevators was out of order.

"This is nice," Mark said.

"They call them lifts," Jule said, causing a man beside her to stare. "Uh…the elevators."

"What do they call them when you're going down?" Mark asked.

On the surface, Suzanne breathed deeply. Late foliage always smelled a little sad and dusty.

They were staying at the Royal National Hotel, a large tourist haven.

"I'm Peter Mansbridge for the National…the ROYAL National," Mark practiced a knockoff Brit accent.

Suzanne would have killed for a chance to take a nap, but Mark was keen on finding a curry place.

"Rooms are not quite ready," settled it, and they dropped their bags and went out walking. They found a tiny closet of a spot with memorabilia on the walls: black and white photos of so-called famous people who'd supposedly dined there.

"That football mega-star couldn't fit through this door," Mark mused.

Celebrities with loud ties, even in black and white.

Suzanne sipped a tepid chai, while Mark and Jule worked on their Bombardiers.

As they sat there, the lights dimmed, like gaslight in an old movie. And it was perfect; the tea just warm; the low-beamed ceiling; the travel photo of India; the pale faces of her friends. She looked from one to the other and felt completely happy.

"I'm glad I'm here," she told the Hope Fiends. "I'm glad we came."

They decided to save the trip to The Tree until morning,

when they would all be fresh. Jule unfolded a brochure she'd picked up at the door. "Oh, look, we're not far from Madame Tussaud's. Want to go and see waxy people?"

Suzanne said no. Mark and Jule admitted they were also beat, so they headed back to the hotel. They hugged and touched heads goodnight, and teetered off to their rooms, Mark and Jule arm in arm down the hall.

Suzanne flipped through the satellite stations, then turned off the remote. She lay on the bed, taking in the strangeness of the place. She'd always done this in any new setting. Aunt Sophie's in the city, her room changes with Annie. The Home. All the moves. Only on her sleeping mat did she know exactly where she was.

Okitsu kagami.

Distant mirror.

Hetsu kagami.

Close…nearby mirror.

She got up and looked at her reflection. Yes. Forty-two. And counting.

•

In the morning, it was much easier without the suitcases. Jule was carrying a shoulder bag, and Suzanne had a small day pack with only the necessities: map, wallet, tissues.

"I can't believe it's happening," she said, which pleased the Hope Fiends.

Back to the Russell Square station and on to Leicester Square, where they'd switch to the Northern Line.

"Remember me?" Jule asked. "Is that what you say at Leicester Square?"

Suzanne smiled. "If you want to."

"Remember me," Jule said.

Remember me, Suzanne breathed.

Walking through the station. Someone was whistling deep in the tunnel. Orpheus, wandering in his earnest quest for Eurydice, the naiad—dyrad?—whom he loved. His music so sweet even stones and trees listened.

"Even the stones and trees," Suzanne whispered, pulled along by the soft whistle.

"What are you on about?" Jule said, taking Suzanne's arm.

"Orpheus. Eurydice. Love."

"Love? Didn't she die?"

"Was dead. But he charmed the Underworld into releasing her."

"Oh, yeah," Jule said. "But...what was it? He wasn't supposed to look back? He had to lead her out of Death but not look back."

"Then he did."

"Yeah, and she was, what, killed again?" Jule asked.

"Hey, if you can be born again..." Mark offered.

"She turned into mist and dissolved back into the Underworld," Suzanne said.

Mark nodded. "Bummer."

•

"All the way to Waterloo on this line, and, no, Suzanne, don't tell me you know a song about it, because I know it, too. Is everything in London named after songs?" Jule asked.

"Waterloo always sounds so...final...when you say it," Mark noted.

"And Elba doesn't?"

"You know, meeting your Waterloo. My cousin went to the University of Waterloo, back in Ontario. His personal Waterloo came in the form of the Brick Brewing Company on King Street."

Suzanne began weaving through the crowd.

"Whoa...what's the rush?" Mark yelled. "Wasn't it you who said the Tree would still be there?"

Sad to see
Them mourning you
When you are here
Within the
Flowers & the Trees.

"Leicester straight down to Waterloo," Mark pointed. Jule got out her city map, and they made Suzanne take off her day pack so they could balance London on her back, tracing the street route to the Tree. Then Suzanne turned away.

Tenkan.

Jule and Mark were still preoccupied with their plans when Suzanne gave them a little wave.

"Oh," Jule caught it. "When we were in Aachen, Germany, we saw these statues all over town, of people holding up their little fingers, their pinkies. What did they call them, Mark? *Klenke.* The finger thing is their special greeting. You can supposedly go all over the world, and if someone else does that signal it means they're from Aachen. Cool, eh?"

Jule held her baby finger up and shook it at Suzanne. Suzanne put up her hand and gestured with the air where her finger used to be.

The Hope Fiends. They would be all right.

•

She pushed her way to the front of the platform. Beside her was a young girl, fussing with a pink purse. She was fifteen or sixteen, her lipstick slightly uneven. She looked like any other girl here, or in Canada, dressed up to go out with friends, or to class for that matter, though she was a little light on books. She noticed Suzanne staring at her and looked away.

•

Suzanne could hear it in the tunnel, the train that would go to Waterloo Station. It sounded the same as all the other trains.

Somebody needed a wash, or a more robust deodorant. Somebody else could have used one less spritz of cologne. But they were all there, waiting. Suzanne looked back once more at Jule and Mark. Jule was pointing over the heads of people, motioning for Suzanne to stand by and wait for them to move closer.

The young girl with the purse had pulled back her hair, freeing her face from its shadow. It was a deliberate gesture, an admirable one, like that of Anne Boleyn, or any of the about-to-be-beheaded queens of the king.

The girl reminded her of Zara. A strange state to live in, middle ground in the Underground, a Middle Earth of confusion and rapture. It will pass, Suzanne wanted to say. Like everything would pass. But the girl saw eternity in these days. She was fiddling with the clasp on her bag. And Suzanne knew for sure. The two of them, not on the edge of an abyss, but on a subway platform, the girl and a middle-aged woman with frizzy hair.

Hey, Fire Engine Sue.

The wheels trilled on the tracks.

People shuffled and moved in close. It was funny how it was sound now, and not sight. So much for visions.

Fire Engine Sue.

We do the best we can with what we've got.

We do. Most of us. Most of the time.

And she remembered her opposite number, the Bearer of Glad Tidings. Where was she?

Suzanne stood exactly on her mark, the girl beside her. Fire Engine Sue glanced over. There was precision in the girl's stance, heat on her brow. The approaching car would be packed. Bottled Londoners, moving from station to station. Hah. *Station to Station*, that was Bowie, not Bolan. Bowie, who went to Bolan's funeral.

Out of the corner of her eye, she could see the pink purse like a little flag. Suzanne took a deep breath. *Kokyu.*

She liked breathing.

Even the curry and leather, the sweat.

She could be in the Indies. Her father's favourite line from *The Mask of Dimitrios,* Peter Lorre sniffing, "Now you won't get to go to the Indies."

And Sidney Greenstreet replying, "There's not enough kindness in the world."

No, Suzanne thought. Not nearly enough. Never enough. But some.

Which was a glad tiding.

Her eyes opened wide.

The purse moved forward. The girl looked down, and a small noise escaped her. Suzanne stepped close as the girl made her move, stretched her arm across the girl's front, her neck, and turned.

Breath throw.

"No!"

An intake of breath as the girl was thrown back against the crowd. An exhalation as the woman fell, leaf-like, in front of the train. The lights flickered and wicked, like electric candles, short candles in the snow on the way to the penguin house.

•

In a park by a tree, people pause and reflect. A flower is placed for the man who died there, another flower for a friend of the couple standing by. In a river on another continent, frogs are slowing down for winter, but there are still children on the banks listening for their call.

Acknowledgements

Anytime a writer has two minutes to rub together and a place to sit and work, it is clear that others have helped to make this happen. These range from institutions and bodies such as the Canada Council, the Ontario Arts Council, and the City of Ottawa, all of which provided grants that allowed me the time to work on the novel. The National Library and Archives of Canada provided me with excellent resources and a study space in which to work. Thanks to Randall Ware, and to the staff in the Reference Section of the National Library.

I would like to thank the De-Ai Aikikai Aikido Club of Ottawa, and in particular Sensei Colin West, Sensei Selena Leclair, Sensei Steve Leclair, and the ever-patient Sensei Dave Foohey, for their instruction and goodwill. A perpetual novice salutes their knowledge and their open spirits. *Domo arigato gozaimasu.*

Thanks to Sylvia McConnell and Allister Thompson for their editorial advice.

Thanks to Frances Hanna for her expertise and guidance.

Thanks to Heather Menzies for the use of her apartment as a writing space, and for trees and conversation. Thanks to Dr. Anna Carlevaris for our steadfast witness of one another's lives. And for her homemade pasta. And I thank my one of a kind family. You make my life make sense, even to me.

Permissions and Notes

Permission to quote from the Japanese and English prayers in *Shinto Norito* (Tenchi Press; Matsuri Foundation. Victoria: Trafford Pub., 2001) courtesy of Shinto priestess Ann Llewellyn Evans.

Permission to quote from T.Rex, "The Planet Queen" courtesy of Lupus Music, Co. Ltd., London.

Several sources were consulted with regard to the Amaterasu-O-Mikami story. Most useful was the book, *Kogoshúi: Gleanings from Ancient Stories,* tr. Genchi Kató (London: Curzon Press, 1926).

The quote from Keats is from Sonnet 52, "When I have fears that I may cease to be."

The Tennyson quote is from the long poem, "The Princess, A Medley".

The St. Augustine quote is from the prayer, "God of Life".

Photo by Ryszard Mrugalski

Rita Donovan was born in Montreal and has lived in Quebec, Alberta, Ontario and Germany. She is the author of seven books, as well as many short stories and essays.

Dark Jewels was first runner-up (to Nino Ricci) in the W.H. Smith/Books in Canada First Novel Award and won the Ottawa-Carleton Book Award. *Daisy Circus* also won the Ottawa-Carleton Book Award. *Landed* won the CAA/Chapters Book Award and was nominated for the Ottawa Book Award, and *The Plague Saint* was nominated for the James Tiptree Award. .

She currently lives in Ottawa, Ontario, with her family, where she writes and teaches.

Printed in the USA
CPSIA information can be obtained
at www.ICGtesting.com
JSHW082201140824
68134JS00014B/352